OPPOSING VIEWPOINTS® SERIES

ChatGPT, AI, and the Future of Writing

Other Books of Related Interest

Opposing Viewpoints Series

Artificial Intelligence
Digital Rights and Privacy
The Future of Higher Education

At Issue Series

The Media's Influence on Society
Populism in the Digital Age
Troll Factories: Russia's Web Brigades

Current Controversies Series

Big Tech and Democracy
The Internet of Things
Media Trustworthiness

"Congress shall make
no law ... abridging
the freedom of speech,
or of the press."

First Amendment to the U.S. Constitution

The basic foundation of our democracy is the First Amendment guarantee of freedom of expression. The Opposing Viewpoints series is dedicated to the concept of this basic freedom and the idea that it is more important to practice it than to enshrine it.

ChatGPT, AI, and the Future of Writing

Avery Elizabeth Hurt, Book Editor

Published in 2025 by Greenhaven Publishing, LLC
2544 Clinton Street,
Buffalo, NY 14224

Copyright © 2025 by Greenhaven Publishing, LLC

First Edition

All rights reserved. No part of this book may be reproduced in any form
without permission in writing from the publisher, except by a reviewer.

Articles in Greenhaven Publishing anthologies are often edited for length to meet page
requirements. In addition, original titles of these works are changed to clearly present
the main thesis and to explicitly indicate the author's opinion. Every effort is made to
ensure that Greenhaven Publishing accurately reflects the original intent of the authors.
Every effort has been made to trace the owners of the copyrighted material.

Cover image: thinkhubstudio/Shutterstock.com

CataloginginPublication Data

Names: Hurt, Avery Elizabeth, editor.
Title: ChatGPT, AI, and the future of writing / edited by Avery Elizabeth Hurt.
Description: First edition. | Buffalo, NY : Greenhaven Publishing, 2025. | Series:
Opposing viewpoints | Includes bibliographical references and index.
Identifiers: ISBN 9781534509771 (pbk.) | ISBN 9781534509788 (library bound)
Subjects: LCSH: ChatGPT. | Artificial intelligence. | Artificial intelligence
Computer programs. | Artificial intelligence--Educational applications. |
Natural language generation (Computer science)--Computer programs.
Classification: LCC QA76.9.N38 C438 2025 | DDC 006.3'5--dc23

Manufactured in the United States of America

Website: http://greenhavenpublishing.com

Contents

The Importance of Opposing Viewpoints	**11**
Introduction	**14**

Chapter 1: Will ChatGPT Take Jobs Away from Writers?

Chapter Preface	**18**
1. ChatGPT Is Impressive, but No Threat to Writers *Marcel Scharth*	**19**
2. ChatGPT Is a Threat to Hollywood Screenwriters *Holly Willis*	**24**
3. ChatGPT's Limitations Will Prevent It from Replacing Human Marketers Anytime Soon *Omar H. Fares*	**31**
4. Writers Must Be Protected from Their Employers, Not Just from AI *Peter Bloom and Pasi Ahonen*	**36**
Periodical and Internet Sources Bibliography	**41**

Chapter 2: Will ChatGPT Benefit Student Writing?

Chapter Preface	**44**
1. ChatGPT Will Change the Classroom, for Good or Ill *Nicole Lazar, James Byrns, Danielle Crowe, Meghan McGinty, Angela Abraham, Mike Guo, Megan Mann, Prithvi Narayanan, Lydia Roberts, Benjamin Sidore, and Maxwell Wager*	**45**
2. We Should Use AI to Change the Way We Assess Students' Work *Sam Illingworth*	**53**
3. ChatGPT Isn't Increasing Cheating *Carrie Spector*	**59**

4. By Taking Over Our Writing, AI-Driven Programs
   Rob Us of the Ability to Think   **64**
   Naomi S. Baron

5. Those Who Worry About ChatGPT Ruining Writing
   Exercises in Schools Miss the Point of Writing   **69**
   Walker Larson

6. The Rise of AI Makes Learning to Write More
   Important than Ever Before   **74**
   Joel Heng Hartse and Taylor Morphett

Periodical and Internet Sources Bibliography   **79**

Chapter 3: Will ChatGPT Help or Harm Journalists and Journalism?

Chapter Preface   **82**

1. ChatGPT for Journalists: Both Useful and Risky   **84**
   Marina Cemaj Hochstein

2. AI Is Creating a Trust Problem for Media Outlets   **89**
   Héloïse Hakimi Le Grand

3. AI Can Create Entire Fake News Sites, and That's a
   Huge Problem   **95**
   Alex Mahadevan

4. News Organizations Are Developing Policies to
   Maintain Journalistic Integrity While Using AI   **101**
   Clark Merrefield

5. Does OpenAI Have a Right to Use Data from
   Journalism to Train ChatGPT?   **111**
   Mike Cook

6. Information from AI Does Not Meet the Standard
   of Trustworthiness for Journalism   **116**
   Blayne Haggart

Periodical and Internet Sources Bibliography   **121**

Chapter 4: Will ChatGPT Help or Harm Creative Writers?

Chapter Preface	**124**
1. Creative Writers Must Learn to Work with ChatGPT *Olivia Atkins*	**125**
2. ChatGPT Does Not Understand Fiction the Way Good Editors Do *Katherine Day, Renée Otmar, Rose Michael, and* *Sharon Mullins*	**134**
3. AI Takes the Soul Out of Creative Writing *C. G. Jones*	**146**
4. AI Won't Mean the Death of the Author, Just the Starvation of the Artist *Terry Flew*	**150**
5. Human Authors Have the Advantage *Millicent Weber*	**155**
Periodical and Internet Sources Bibliography	**162**
For Further Discussion	**164**
Organizations to Contact	**167**
Bibliography of Books	**171**
Index	**173**

| 10

The Importance of Opposing Viewpoints

Perhaps every generation experiences a period in time in which the populace seems especially polarized, starkly divided on the important issues of the day and gravitating toward the far ends of the political spectrum and away from a consensus-facilitating middle ground. The world that today's students are growing up in and that they will soon enter into as active and engaged citizens is deeply fragmented in just this way. Issues relating to terrorism, immigration, women's rights, minority rights, race relations, health care, taxation, wealth and poverty, the environment, policing, military intervention, the proper role of government—in some ways, perennial issues that are freshly and uniquely urgent and vital with each new generation—are currently roiling the world.

If we are to foster a knowledgeable, responsible, active, and engaged citizenry among today's youth, we must provide them with the intellectual, interpretive, and critical-thinking tools and experience necessary to make sense of the world around them and of the all-important debates and arguments that inform it. After all, the outcome of these debates will in large measure determine the future course, prospects, and outcomes of the world and its peoples, particularly its youth. If they are to become successful members of society and productive and informed citizens, students need to learn how to evaluate the strengths and weaknesses of someone else's arguments, how to sift fact from opinion and fallacy, and how to test the relative merits and validity of their own opinions against the known facts and the best possible available information. The landmark series Opposing Viewpoints has been providing students with just such critical-thinking skills and exposure to the debates surrounding society's most urgent contemporary issues for many years, and it continues to serve this essential role with undiminished commitment, care, and rigor.

The key to the series's success in achieving its goal of sharpening students' critical-thinking and analytic skills resides in its title—

ChatGPT, AI, and the Future of Writing

Opposing Viewpoints. In every intriguing, compelling, and engaging volume of this series, readers are presented with the widest possible spectrum of distinct viewpoints, expert opinions, and informed argumentation and commentary, supplied by some of today's leading academics, thinkers, analysts, politicians, policy makers, economists, activists, change agents, and advocates. Every opinion and argument anthologized here is presented objectively and accorded respect. There is no editorializing in any introductory text or in the arrangement and order of the pieces. No piece is included as a "straw man," an easy ideological target for cheap point-scoring. As wide and inclusive a range of viewpoints as possible is offered, with no privileging of one particular political ideology or cultural perspective over another. It is left to each individual reader to evaluate the relative merits of each argument—as he or she sees it, and with the use of ever-growing critical-thinking skills—and grapple with his or her own assumptions, beliefs, and perspectives to determine how convincing or successful any given argument is and how the reader's own stance on the issue may be modified or altered in response to it.

This process is facilitated and supported by volume, chapter, and selection introductions that provide readers with the essential context they need to begin engaging with the spotlighted issues, with the debates surrounding them, and with their own perhaps shifting or nascent opinions on them. In addition, guided reading and discussion questions encourage readers to determine the authors' point of view and purpose, interrogate and analyze the various arguments and their rhetoric and structure, evaluate the arguments' strengths and weaknesses, test their claims against available facts and evidence, judge the validity of the reasoning, and bring into clearer, sharper focus the reader's own beliefs and conclusions and how they may differ from or align with those in the collection or those of their classmates.

Research has shown that reading comprehension skills improve dramatically when students are provided with compelling, intriguing, and relevant "discussable" texts. The subject matter of these collections could not be more compelling, intriguing, or urgently relevant to today's students and the world they are poised to inherit. The anthologized articles and the reading and discussion questions that are included with them also provide the basis for stimulating, lively, and passionate classroom debates. Students who are compelled to anticipate objections to their own argument and identify the flaws in those of an opponent read more carefully, think more critically, and steep themselves in relevant context, facts, and information more thoroughly. In short, using discussable text of the kind provided by every single volume in the Opposing Viewpoints series encourages close reading, facilitates reading comprehension, fosters research, strengthens critical thinking, and greatly enlivens and energizes classroom discussion and participation. The entire learning process is deepened, extended, and strengthened.

For all of these reasons, Opposing Viewpoints continues to be exactly the right resource at exactly the right time—when we most need to provide readers with the critical-thinking tools and skills that will not only serve them well in school but also in their careers and their daily lives as decision-making family members, community members, and citizens. This series encourages respectful engagement with and analysis of opposing viewpoints and fosters a resulting increase in the strength and rigor of one's own opinions and stances. As such, it helps make readers "future ready," and that readiness will pay rich dividends for the readers themselves, for the citizenry, for our society, and for the world at large.

Introduction

> *"There is a long tradition of techno-gloom with regard to reading and writing: the internet, mass broadcast media, the novel form, the printing press, the act of writing itself."*
>
> —Millicent Weber,
> *Australian data science
> and literature researcher*

It's almost de rigueur that in any article about ChatGPT, the first paragraph or so is written by the AI. Well, don't worry. You haven't been duped here. The intelligence behind the introduction you're now reading is, for better or worse, entirely human. However, the impact of ChatGPT on all forms of writing and on the publishing industry is enormous.

Disruptions to the practice of writing are nothing new, of course. In fact, at one time the very act of writing was new and controversial. In *Phaedrus*, one of the dialogues of Plato from around 370 BCE, Socrates argues that the then-newfangled practice of writing would be a disaster for humanity. If people began writing things down rather than sharing stories and information orally the way they always had, their memories would atrophy. Writing would cause them to forget rather than learn. And indeed, in some ways Socrates was correct. We moderns aren't very good at memorizing epic poems and philosophical treatises. But we do have in our books and in our libraries and even on our phones a wealth of information and literature that Socrates could never have dreamed of.

Introduction

Technological changes continued. At first, most were met with at least suspicion, if not outright hostility. Quills were displaced by fountain pens, fountain pens by ballpoints. Then typewriters came along, only to be replaced by word processors. Until recently, the most disruptive technology in the history of writing was the printing press, which made it possible for books, newspapers, and magazines—in fact, all forms of written material—to reach everyone, not only the rich or well connected. That certainly changed the world.

Now we have ChatGPT, a chatbot based on a Large Language Model (LLM) of artificial intelligence. ChatGPT basically does nothing more sophisticated than assemble enormous amounts of written material from books and websites. Then it predicts the words that are most likely to follow any given word or phrase. Yet from this simple premise, it has been able to not only chat convincingly with humans, but to write. It can produce everything from short blog posts to complete novels. And that may be more disruptive than even the printing press.

In this volume, writers from many different backgrounds explore the potential risks and benefits to writers and writing posed by ChatGPT. The first chapter looks at all types of writing and asks if this new technology will put writers out of work. It very well may, some of the authors here say. But the problem is more complex than just the arrival of a new technology. The current business model of magazines and newspapers make the issue especially thorny.

In the second chapter the authors zero in on the effect of ChatGPT on students. Will this type of AI transform learning and teaching? Will it make it easier for students to cheat? One thing is clear: education will never be quite the same now that ChatGPT has arrived in the classroom.

Journalism is another area where ChatGPT is changing everything. In the third chapter, the viewpoints look closely at how ChatGPT might make life easier for journalists. But they also

ChatGPT, AI, and the Future of Writing

look at how it might not only take journalists' jobs, but ruin the practice of journalism.

The final chapter is about creative writing. ChatGPT can write novels. Does this mean the death of the author? Several of the authors here seem to think so. Others are hopeful that readers will want to engage with a human author rather than with a chatbot, offering some hope for creative writers.

This latest revolution in writing has only just begun, and we can't know how it will turn out. But the authors in *Opposing Viewpoints: ChatGPT, AI, and the Future of Writing* offer sometimes hopeful, sometimes frightening, but always insightful takes on the future of literature in a world where chatbots can write.

CHAPTER 1

Will ChatGPT Take Jobs Away from Writers?

Chapter Preface

On November 30, 2022, OpenAI released ChatGPT and amazed the world. The large language model AI could chat with humans almost as easily as another human. That was cool. It could also put together a decent piece of writing. That, at least for people who make their living writing, was terrifying. Writers suddenly saw their jobs going the way of those of elevator attendants and switchboard operators. But will programs like ChatGPT really put writers out of work? The authors here take on that question. Some are reassuring; others urge caution. One author reports on places where it is already happening.

The first viewpoint begins by explaining what ChatGPT is and what it does. While acknowledging that the AI is pretty amazing, the author argues that it has neither the creativity nor the critical thinking skills to replace humans—at least not yet. The next two viewpoints look at the impact ChatGPT may have on two fields that are currently dependent on writers—screenwriting and marketing. While AI has not yet assumed a major role in either field, its potential to disrupt these careers and potentially replace human writers is explored. The final viewpoint considers the potential negative impacts AI could have on professional writers and ways in which it may be possible to prevent this from becoming an issue.

It's too early to know what ChatGPT will and will not be able to do. Perhaps it will become more creative and figure out how to think critically. Maybe it will stop plagiarizing the work of others and learn to produce original writing. Meanwhile the human writers represented here are scrambling to figure out how best to cope with this exciting, but potentially threatening, technology.

VIEWPOINT 1

> *"One practical problem is that ChatGPT's knowledge is static; it doesn't access new information in real time."*

ChatGPT Is Impressive, but No Threat to Writers

Marcel Scharth

Written the week ChatGPT was released in November 2022, this viewpoint by Marcel Scharth explains what the program is and what it can do. He also assures readers that ChatGPT does not have the creativity or critical thinking skills to replace human writers. ChatGPT is an impressive and useful tool, and its ability to reproduce human communication could allow it to take the place of humans in replacing some tasks, but it will not be able to replace the original thinking of humans. Marcel Scharth is a lecturer in business analytics at the University of Sydney in Australia.

As you read, consider the following questions:

1. What material does OpenAI use to train ChatGPT?

"The ChatGPT chatbot is blowing people away with its writing skills. An expert explains why it's so impressive," by Marcel Scharth, The Conversation, December 6, 2022, https://theconversation.com/the-chatgpt-chatbot-is-blowing-people-away-with-its-writing-skills-an-expert-explains-why-its-so-impressive-195908. Licensed under CC BY-ND 4.0 International.

19 |

2. What problems with ChatGPT does Scharth mention here that he says need addressing?
3. How might ChatGPT be an alternative to Google?

We've all had some kind of interaction with a chatbot. It's usually a little pop-up in the corner of a website, offering customer support—often clunky to navigate—and almost always frustratingly non-specific.

But imagine a chatbot, enhanced by artificial intelligence (AI), that can not only expertly answer your questions, but also write stories, give life advice, even compose poems and code computer programs.

It seems ChatGPT, a chatbot released last week by OpenAI, is delivering on these outcomes. It has generated much excitement, and some have gone as far as to suggest it could signal a future in which AI has dominion over human content producers.

What has ChatGPT done to herald such claims? And how might it (and its future iterations) become indispensable in our daily lives?

What Can ChatGPT Do?

ChatGPT builds on OpenAI's previous text generator, GPT-3. OpenAI builds its text-generating models by using machine-learning algorithms to process vast amounts of text data, including books, news articles, Wikipedia pages and millions of websites.

By ingesting such large volumes of data, the models learn the complex patterns and structure of language and acquire the ability to interpret the desired outcome of a user's request.

ChatGPT can build a sophisticated and abstract representation of the knowledge in the training data, which it draws on to produce outputs. This is why it writes relevant content, and doesn't just spout grammatically correct nonsense.

While GPT-3 was designed to continue a text prompt, ChatGPT is optimised to conversationally engage, answer questions and be helpful. Here's an example:

ChatGPT immediately grabbed my attention by correctly answering exam questions I've asked my undergraduate and postgraduate students, including questions requiring coding skills. Other academics have had similar results.

In general, it can provide genuinely informative and helpful explanations on a broad range of topics.

ChatGPT is also potentially useful as a writing assistant. It does a decent job drafting text and coming up with seemingly "original" ideas.

The Power of Feedback

Why does ChatGPT seem so much more capable than some of its past counterparts? A lot of this probably comes down to how it was trained.

During its development ChatGPT was shown conversations between human AI trainers to demonstrate desired behaviour. Although there's a similar model trained in this way, called InstructGPT, ChatGPT is the first popular model to use this method.

And it seems to have given it a huge leg-up. Incorporating human feedback has helped steer ChatGPT in the direction of producing more helpful responses and rejecting inappropriate requests.

Refusing to entertain inappropriate inputs is a particularly big step towards improving the safety of AI text generators, which can otherwise produce harmful content, including bias and stereotypes, as well as fake news, spam, propaganda and false reviews.

Past text-generating models have been criticised for regurgitating gender, racial and cultural biases contained in training data. In some cases, ChatGPT successfully avoids reinforcing such stereotypes.

Nevertheless, users have already found ways to evade its existing safeguards and produce biased responses.

ChatGPT, AI, and the Future of Writing

The fact that the system often accepts requests to write fake content is further proof that it needs refinement.

Overcoming Limitations

ChatGPT is arguably one of the most promising AI text generators, but it's not free from errors and limitations. For instance, programming advice platform Stack Overflow temporarily banned answers by the chatbot for a lack of accuracy.

One practical problem is that ChatGPT's knowledge is static; it doesn't access new information in real time.

However, its interface does allow users to give feedback on the model's performance by indicating ideal answers, and reporting harmful, false or unhelpful responses.

OpenAI intends to address existing problems by incorporating this feedback into the system. The more feedback users provide, the more likely ChatGPT will be to decline requests leading to an undesirable output.

One possible improvement could come from adding a "confidence indicator" feature based on user feedback. This tool, which could be built on top of ChatGPT, would indicate the model's confidence in the information it provides—leaving it to the user to decide whether they use it or not. Some question-answering systems already do this.

A New Tool, but Not a Human Replacement

Despite its limitations, ChatGPT works surprisingly well for a prototype.

From a research point of view, it marks an advancement in the development and deployment of human-aligned AI systems. On the practical side, it's already effective enough to have some everyday applications.

It could, for instance, be used as an alternative to Google. While a Google search requires you to sift through a number of websites and dig deeper yet to find the desired information, ChatGPT directly answers your question—and often does this well.

Also, with feedback from users and a more powerful GPT-4 model coming up, ChatGPT may significantly improve in the future. As ChatGPT and other similar chatbots become more popular, they'll likely have applications in areas such as education and customer service.

However, while ChatGPT may end up performing some tasks traditionally done by people, there's no sign it will replace professional writers any time soon.

While they may impress us with their abilities and even their apparent creativity, AI systems remain a reflection of their training data—and do not have the same capacity for originality and critical thinking as humans do.

VIEWPOINT 2

> *"Writers fear that, at best, they will be hired to edit screenplays drafted by AI. They fear that their creative work will be swallowed whole into databases as the fodder for writing tools to sample."*

ChatGPT Is a Threat to Hollywood Screenwriters

Holly Willis

In this viewpoint, Holly Willis discusses the 2023 strikes by the Writers Guild of America and the Screen Actors Guild, groups that worried major Hollywood studios would use generative AI like ChatGPT to take their jobs or exploit them. Screenwriters worry that ChatGPT could be used to write screenplays, leaving human screenwriters with just the work of editing these AI-generated pieces. They are also anxious that their creative work will be sampled by AI or that their jobs will be replaced by people who know how to effectively prompt AI to generate screenplays. However, Willis asserts that it is possible for AI to be used in a way that collaborates with writers to help improve their work, especially if writers were involved in the creation of these tools. Holly Willis is a professor of cinematic arts at the University of Southern California.

"What Are Hollywood Actors and Writers Afraid Of? A Cinema Scholar Explains How AI Is Upending the Movie and TV Business," by Holly Willis, The Conversation, August 7, 2023, https://theconversation.com/what-are-hollywood-actors-and-writers-afraid-of-a-cinema-scholar-explains-how-ai-is-upending-the-movie-and-tv-business-210360. Licensed under CC BY-ND 4.0 International.

Will ChatGPT Take Jobs Away from Writers?

As you read, consider the following questions:

1. How did Willis use ChatGPT to create a short film about Barbie and Ken?
2. What examples does Willis provide of studios using AI?
3. According to this viewpoint, how could technological development be improved for writers and other creative professionals?

The bitter conflict between actors, writers and other creative professionals and the major movie and TV studios represents a flashpoint in the radical transformation roiling the entertainment industry. The ongoing strikes by the Writers Guild of America and the Screen Actors Guild were sparked in part by artificial intelligence and its use in the movie industry.

Both actors and writers fear that the major studios, including Amazon/MGM, Apple, Disney/ABC/Fox, NBCUniversal, Netflix, Paramount/CBS, Sony, Warner Bros. and HBO, will use generative AI to exploit them. Generative AI is a form of artificial intelligence that learns from text and images to automatically produce new written and visual works.

So what specifically are the writers and actors afraid of? I'm a professor of cinematic arts. I conducted a brief exercise that illustrates the answer.

I typed the following sentence into ChatGPT: Create a script for a 5-minute film featuring Barbie and Ken. In seconds, a script appeared.

Next, I asked for a shot list, a breakdown of every camera shot needed for the film. Again, a response appeared almost instantly, featuring not only a "montage of fun activities," but also a fancy flashback sequence. The closing line suggested a wide shot showing "Barbie and Ken walking away from the beach together, hand in hand."

Next, on a text-to-video platform, I typed these words into a box labeled "Prompt": "Cinematic movie shot of Margot Robbie

25 |

ChatGPT, AI, and the Future of Writing

as Barbie walking near the beach, early morning light, pink sun rays illuminating the screen, tall green grass, photographic detail, film grain."

About a minute later, a 3-second video appeared. It showed a svelte blond woman walking on the beach. Is it Margot Robbie? Is it Barbie? It's hard to say. I decided to add my own face in place of Robbie's just for fun, and in seconds, I've made the swap.

I now have a moving image clip on my desktop that I can add to the script and shot list, and I'm well on my way to crafting a short film starring someone sort of like Margot Robbie as Barbie.

The Fear

None of this material is particularly good. The script lacks tension and poetic grace. The shot list is uninspired. And the video is just plain weird-looking.

However, the ability for anyone—amateurs and professionals alike—to create a screenplay and conjure the likeness of an existing actor means that the skills once specific to writers and the likeness that an actor once could uniquely call his or her own are now readily available—with questionable quality, to be sure—to anyone with access to these free online tools.

Given the rate of technological change, the quality of all this material created through generative AI is destined to improve visually, not only for people like me and social media creatives globally, but possibly for the studios, which are likely to have access to much more powerful computers. Further, these separate steps—preproduction, screenwriting, production, postproduction—could be absorbed into a streamlined prompting system that bears little resemblance to today's art and craft of moviemaking.

Writers fear that, at best, they will be hired to edit screenplays drafted by AI. They fear that their creative work will be swallowed whole into databases as the fodder for writing tools to sample. And they fear that their specific expertise will be pushed aside in favor of "prompt engineers," or those skilled at working with AI tools.

| 26

And actors fret that they will be forced to sell their likeness once, only to see it used over and over by studios. They fear that deepfake technologies will become the norm, and real, live actors won't be needed at all. And they worry that not only their bodies but their voices will be taken, synthesized and reused without continued compensation. And all of this is on top of dwindling incomes for the vast majority of actors.

On the Road to the AI Future

Are their fears justified? Sort of. In June 2023, Marvel showcased titles—opening sequences with episode names—for the series *Secret Invasion* on Disney+ that were created in part with AI tools. The use of AI by a major studio sparked controversy due in part to the timing and fears about AI displacing people from their jobs. Further, series director and executive producer Ali Selim's tone-deaf description of the use of AI only added to the sense that there is little concern at all about those fears.

Then on July 26, software developer Nicholas Neubert posted a 48-second trailer for a sci-fi film made with images made by AI image generator Midjourney and motion created by Runway's image-to-motion generator, Gen-2. It looks terrific. No screenwriter was hired. No actors were used.

In addition, earlier this month, a company called Fable released Showrunner AI, which is designed to allow users to submit images and voices, along with a brief prompt. The tool responds by creating entire episodes that include the user.

The creators have been using *South Park* as their sample, and they have presented plausible new episodes of the show that integrate viewers as characters in the story. The idea is to create a new form of audience engagement. However, for both writers and actors, Showrunner AI must be chilling indeed.

Finally, Volkswagen recently produced a commercial that features an AI reincarnation of Brazilian musician Elis Regina, who died in 1982. Directed by Dulcidio Caldeira, it shows the musician as she appears to sing a duet with her daughter. For

ChatGPT, AI, and the Future of Writing

ChatGPT Makes Life Easier for Writers, but Could Take Their Jobs

ChatGPT and its AI powers could help writers and office workers improve their writing quality and decrease the time spent on tasks, cutting out busy work in favor of better, more productive work. However, the MIT study that suggested these conclusions also warned that employers could use AI to increase layoffs.

The paper, "Experimental Evidence on the Productivity Effects of Generative Artificial Intelligence" by Shakked Noy and Whitney Zhang of the economics department at MIT, is considered a working paper and has not been peer-reviewed. Still, the conclusions it found about ChatGPT's AI chatbot technology are both fascinating—and troubling. . . .

The two doctoral students split 444 college-educated professionals into two groups, and assigned them to write press releases, email, short reports, and analysis plans—a normal workday for many people. One of the groups was allowed to use a text editor. The other was trained and allowed to use ChatGPT to do the work for them. The output was rated, assigned a value score, and those with the highest score were paid an actual (though nominal) amount of money for their high scores, pushing them to deliver their best work.

some, the song was a beautiful revelation, crafting a poignant mother-daughter reunion.

However, for others, the AI regeneration of someone who has died prompts worries about how one's likeness might be used after death. What if you are morally opposed to a particular film project, TV show or commercial? How will actors—and others—be able to retain control?

Keeping Actors and Writers in Control

Writers' and actors' fears could be assuaged if the entertainment industry developed a convincing and inclusive vision that acknowledges advances in AI, but that collaborates with writers and

The study found that those who used ChatGPT cut the time needed to complete the tasks by almost half (30 minutes to about 17 minutes). The quality of the work also increased, with the grades assigned by the evaluators (on a 1-7 scale) rising from 4 to about 4.7. Those who used the text editor saw a slight decrease in time spent but also a decrease in the quality of the work.

[...]

The study participants also reported that using ChatGPT significantly increased their job satisfaction, eliminating the "busy work" that can plague some tasks . . . . But those tested also indicated that ChatGPT didn't always know as much as they did.

The other problem, the authors noted—remember, they're economists—is that employers may start recognizing the value of ChatGPT, too. That may put worker jobs in jeopardy.

"At the aggregate level, ChatGPT substantially compresses the productivity distribution, reducing inequality," Noy and Zhang wrote. "It is also already being used by many workers in their real jobs. The experimental evidence suggests that ChatGPT largely substitutes for worker effort rather than complementing workers' skills, potentially causing a decrease in demand for workers, with adverse distributional effects as capital owners gain at the expense of workers."

"ChatGPT's AI powers make better writers" by Mark Hachman. IDG Communications, Inc. March 14, 2023.

actors, not to mention cinematographers, directors, art designers and others, as partners.

At the moment, developers are rapidly building and improving AI tools. Production companies are likely to use them to dramatically cut costs, which will contribute to a massive shift toward a gig-oriented economy. If the dismissive attitude toward writers and actors held by many of the major studios continues, not only will there be little consideration of the needs of writers and actors, but technology development will lead the conversation.

However, what if the tools were designed with the participation of informed actors and writers? What kind of tool would an actor create? What would a writer create? What sorts of conditions

ChatGPT, AI, and the Future of Writing

regarding intellectual property, copyright and creativity would developers consider? And what sort of inclusive, forward-looking, creative cinematic ecosystem might evolve? Answering these questions could give actors and writers the assurances they seek and help the industry adapt in the age of AI.

VIEWPOINT 3

> *"ChatGPT could provide creative content and support content ideation. However, the human factor is still essential for examining outputs and creating marketing messages that are consistent with a firm's business strategy and vision."*

ChatGPT's Limitations Will Prevent It from Replacing Human Marketers Anytime Soon

Omar H. Fares

In this viewpoint, Omar H. Fares examines the impact ChatGPT could have on marketing careers. He begins by explaining why ChatGPT has been such a gamechanger in a way that earlier chatbots have not. However, he also explains that there usually is a hype cycle surrounding new technologies, and that marketers should not overestimate ChatGPT's potential based on its current hype. He argues that it could be used to enhance and edit written work and generate emails and social media posts, but because ChatGPT does not have the accuracy, creativity, or emotional intelligence of humans, it will not be able to replace humans who work in marketing. Omar H. Fares is a lecturer in the Ted Rogers School of Retail Management at Toronto Metropolitan University.

"ChatGPT Could Be a Gamechanger for Marketers, but It Won't Replace Humans Any Time Soon," by Omar H. Fares, The Conversation, January 22, 2023, https://theconversation.com/chatgpt-could-be-a-game-changer-for-marketers-but-it-wont-replace-humans-any-time-soon-198053. Licensed under CC BY-ND 4.0 International.

ChatGPT, AI, and the Future of Writing

As you read, consider the following questions:

1. According to Fares, what sets ChatGPT apart from other chatbots?
2. What is Gartner's hype cycle?
3. Why does Fares argue that the human factor is still essential to successful marketing?

The recent release of the ChatGPT chatbot in November 2022 has generated significant public interest. In essence, ChatGPT is an AI-powered chatbot allowing users to simulate human-like conversations with an AI.

GPT stands for Generative Pre-trained Transformer, a language processing model developed by the American artificial intelligence company OpenAI. The GPT language model uses deep learning to produce human-like responses. Deep learning is a branch of machine learning that involves training artificial neural networks to mimic the complexity of the human brain, to produce human-like responses.

ChatGPT has a user-friendly interface that utilizes this technology, allowing users to interact with it in a conversational manner.

In light of this new technology, businesses and consumers alike have shown great interest in how such an innovation could revolutionize marketing strategies and customer experiences.

What's So Special About ChatGPT?

What sets ChatGPT apart from other chatbots is the size of its dataset. Chatbots are usually trained on a smaller dataset in a rule-based manner designed to answer specific questions and conduct certain tasks.

ChatGPT, on the other hand, is trained on a huge dataset—175 billion parameters and 570 gigabytes—and is able to perform a range of tasks in different fields and industries. 570GB is equivalent to over 385 million pages on Microsoft Word.

Given the amount of the data, ChatGPT can carry out different language-related activities which includes answering questions in different fields and sectors, providing answers in different languages and generating content.

Friend or Foe to Marketers?

While ChatGPT may be a tremendous tool for marketers, it is important to understand the realistic possibilities and expectations of it to get the most value from it.

Traditionally, with the emergence of new technologies, consumers tend to go through Gartner's hype cycle. In essence, Gartner's cycle explains the process people go through when adopting a new technology.

The cycle starts with the innovation trigger and peak of inflated triggers stages when consumers get enthusiastic about new technology and expectations start to build. Then consumers realize the pitfalls of the technology, creating a gap between expectations and reality. This is called the trough of disillusionment.

This is followed by the slope of enlightenment when consumers start to understand the technology and use it more appropriately and reasonably. Finally, the technology becomes widely adopted and used as intended during the plateau of productivity stage.

With the current public excitement surrounding ChatGPT, we appear to be nearing the peak of inflated triggers stage. It's important for marketers to set realistic expectations for consumers and navigate the integration of ChatGPT to mitigate the effects of the trough of disillusionment stage.

Possibilities of ChatGPT

In its current form, ChatGPT cannot replace the human factor in marketing, but it could support content creation, enhance customer service, automate repetitive tasks and support data analysis.

- **Supporting content creation:** Marketers may use ChatGPT to enhance existing content by using it to edit written work, make suggestions, summarize ideas and improve overall copy readability. Additionally, ChatGPT may enhance search engine optimization strategy by examining ideal keywords and tags.

- **Enhancing customer service:** Businesses may train ChatGPT to respond to frequently asked questions and interact with customers in a human-like conversation. Rather than replacing the human factor, ChatGPT could provide 24/7 customer support. This could optimize business resources and enhance internal processes by leaving high-impact and sensitive tasks to humans. ChatGPT can also be trained in different languages, further enhancing customer experience and satisfaction.
- **Automating repetitive marketing tasks:** According to a 2015 HubSpot report, marketers spent a significant amount of their time on repetitive tasks, such as sending emails and creating social media posts. While part of that challenge has been addressed with customer relationship management software, ChatGPT may enhance this by providing an added layer of personalization through the generation of creative content.

Additionally, ChatGPT may be helpful in other tasks, such as product descriptions. With access to a wealth of data, ChatGPT would be able to frequently update and adjust product descriptions, allowing marketers to focus on higher-impact tasks.

Limitations of ChatGPT

While the wide range of possibilities for enhancing marketing processes with ChatGPT are enticing, it is important for businesses to know about some key limitations and when to limit or avoid using ChatGPT in business operations.

- **Emotional intelligence:** ChatGPT provides a state of the art human-like response and content. However, it is important to be aware that the tool is only human-like. Similar to traditional challenges with chatbots, the degree of human-likeness will be essential for process enhancement and content creation. Marketers could use ChatGPT to enhance customer experience, but without humans to provide relevancy, character, experience and personal connection, it will be challenging to fully capitalize on ChatGPT. Relying on ChatGPT to build customer connections and engagement without the involvement of humans may diminish meaningful customer connection instead of enhancing it.

- **Accuracy:** While the marketing content may appear logical, it is important to note that ChatGPT is not error free and may provide incorrect and illogical answers. Marketers need to review and validate the content generated by ChatGPT to avoid possible errors and ensure consistency with brand message and image.
- **Creativity:** Relying on ChatGPT for creative content may cause short- and long-term challenges. ChatGPT lacks the lived experience of individuals and understanding the complexity of human nature. Over-relying on ChatGPT may limit creative abilities, so it should be used to support ideation and enhance existing content while still allowing room for human creativity.

Humans Are Irreplaceable

While ChatGPT has the potential to enhance marketing effectiveness, businesses should only use the technology as a tool to assist humans, not replace them. ChatGPT could provide creative content and support content ideation. However, the human factor is still essential for examining outputs and creating marketing messages that are consistent with a firm's business strategy and vision.

A business that does not have a strong marketing strategy before integrating ChatGPT remains at a competitive disadvantage. However, with appropriate marketing strategies and plans, ChatGPT could effectively enhance and support existing marketing processes.

VIEWPOINT 4

> *"It's also important to recognize that the dangers are being aggravated by companies' focus on maximising profits and productivity."*

Writers Must Be Protected from Their Employers, Not Just from AI

Peter Bloom and Pasi Ahonen

In this viewpoint, Peter Bloom and Pasi Ahonen suggest that regulations to protect workers might be needed to prevent ChatGPT from becoming a "nightmare" for professional writers. The authors suggest that the use of ChatGPT could be beneficial by helping speed up the writing process, which could make writing more accessible in an environment that favors the speed of writers. However, they also claim that it could put some writers out of work and pressure those who do retain their jobs to be more productive. In order for ChatGPT to have a positive impact on workplaces, regulation should be used to prevent the exploitation of workers. Peter Bloom is a professor of management at the University of Essex in England. Pasi Ahonen is a senior lecturer in management and marketing at the University of Essex.

"ChatGPT: how to prevent it becoming a nightmare for professional writers" by Peter Bloom and Pasi Ahonen, The Conversation, March 1, 2023, https://theconversation.com/chatgpt-how-to-prevent-it-becoming-a-nightmare-for-professional-writers-200661. Licensed under CC BY-ND 4.0 International.

Will ChatGPT Take Jobs Away from Writers?

As you read, consider the following questions:

1. What technologies do the authors mention that have improved the working lives of writers over the course of history?
2. Why would ChatGPT be an advantage to writers working in a language not native to them?
3. What intellectual property issues are raised by ChatGPT and similar AI?

Nearly half of white-collar professionals have tried using ChatGPT to help with their work, according to a recent survey of more than 10,000 people at blue chips such as Google, JP Morgan and McKinsey. That's staggering, considering the AI chatbot was only released to the public in November. It's potentially very exciting for the future of work, but it also brings serious risks.

ChatGPT and other imminent rivals are part of a long history of technologies geared to reducing the labour of writing. These range from the printing press to the telegram, the typewriter, word processors and personal computing.

AI chatbots can help overcome human limitations, including speed, foreign languages and writer's block—potentially helping with everything from writing emails to reports and articles to marketing campaigns. It's a fascinating trans-human relationship in which the AI uses past human-produced texts to inform and shape the writing of new texts by other humans.

Jobs involving significant amounts of writing will inevitably be affected most, such as journalists, academic researchers and policy analysts. In all cases, AI chatbots could allow for new knowledge and ideas to be disseminated more rapidly. Certainly it could lead to weaker, less useful writing, but if used to create a structure that is thoroughly edited by the writer using their own original ideas, it could be very beneficial.

Also, some people have a competitive advantage at writing not because their ideas are better but because they are just faster.

ChatGPT, AI, and the Future of Writing

This is often because they are writing in their first language, due to nothing more than historical coincidence. AI chatbots could therefore help make writing more inclusive and accessible.

Downsides

On the other hand, there are worries that ChatGPT and its competitors could steal many people's jobs, especially in traditional white collar professions, though it's very difficult to say at this stage how many people will be affected. For example Mihir Shukla, CEO and founder of California-based software company Automation Anywhere, thinks that "anywhere from 15% to 70% of all the work we do in front of the computer could be automated." On the other hand a recent McKinsey report suggests that only about 9% of people will have to change careers. Even so, that's a lot of people. Lower to mid-level employees are likely to be the ones most affected.

Linked to possible job losses is the danger that employers will use these technologies to justify cost savings by making existing workers use these tools "to do more with less." Employers have historically used labor-saving devices to maximise productivity, making people work harder, not smarter or better. Computers and emails, for example, have made work never-ending for many people.

Employees could now therefore end up being pressured to produce more work. Yet this risks missing the real leap in productivity that AI could bring about. If used correctly, AI chatbots could free up employees to have more time to produce high-quality, original work.

There are additionally concerns about the human cost of creating AI chatbots. Kenyan workers, for instance, were paid between US$1 and US$2 (80 pence to £1.60) per hour to train OpenAI's GPT-3 model, on which ChatGPT is based. Their brief was to make it less toxic by labelling thousands of samples of potentially offensive text so that the platform could learn to detect violent, racist and sexist language. This was so traumatic for the workers that the contractor nearly brought the project to an early end. Unfortunately, there's likely to be much more of this kind of work to come.

Finally, AI chatbots raise fascinating intellectual property issues. In particular, it's not clear who owns the work they produce. This could make it harder for companies or freelancers to protect their own output, while also potentially exposing them to copyright infringement claims from someone who owned the writing that seems to have been reproduced by the AI chatbot. It's a complex area and it very much remains to be seen by courts will handle test cases.

It also raises questions about situations where the ownership of a piece of work is already in a grey area. While an employer will often own an employee's written work, this has not traditionally been the case with university academics. Now, however, universities are seeking to use their power as employers to often be the first owners of academics' published research. If they succeed, they could then put pressure on academics to use AI chatbots to increase their level of research output.

Worker-Friendly AI?

One way of dealing with the dangers of heavier workloads is through regulation. At this stage, however we worry that the authorities will set more of an aspirational "ceiling" for what employers should aim to do for employees rather than a clearly regulated and enforced "floor" for ensuring decent work.

We must start developing basic standards to limit the potential for exploiting workers. This could include caps on the amount of AI-assisted written work that companies can expect of individuals, for instance. There's clearly also an important role for raising employers' awareness about the potential harms and benefits from these technologies.

It's also important to recognise that the dangers are being aggravated by companies' focus on maximising profits and productivity. This points to the need for more alternative work environments where the emphasis is on providing workers with

ChatGPT, AI, and the Future of Writing

a good quality of life. The OECD has for instance been promoting the "social economy," which encompasses worker and community-owned cooperatives. In such workplaces, tools such as ChatGPT have the potential to be more beneficial than threatening.

The good news is that there is probably a narrow window before these technologies transform workplaces. We tried using ChatGPT to write this article and didn't find it particularly useful—though that may partly reflect our own inexperience at prompting the chatbot. Now is the time to recognize where this is heading and get the world up to speed. A year or two from now, workplaces could look very different.

Periodical and Internet Sources Bibliography

The following articles have been selected to supplement the diverse views presented in this chapter.

Ian Bogost, "ChatGPT Is Dumber Than You Think," the *Atlantic*, December 7, 2022. https://www.theatlantic.com/technology/archive/2022/12/chatgpt-openai-artificial-intelligence-writing-ethics/672386/.

Tom Comitta, "*Death of an Author* Prophesies the Future of AI Novels," *Wired*, May 9, 2023. https://www.wired.com/story/death-of-an-author-ai-book-review/.

Katherine Fidler, "ChatGPT Wrote a Novel Called *Death Of An Author*—but It's Not Making a Point," *Metro*, May 15, 2023. https://metro.co.uk/2023/05/15/chatgpt-wrote-a-novel-called-death-of-an-author-18786874/.

Giancarlo Ghedini, "ChatGPT: A Writer's Best Friend...for Now," *Writer's Digest*, June 29, 2023. https://www.writersdigest.com/be-inspired/chatgpt-a-writers-best-friend-for-now.

Randall Horton, "Are We Witnessing the Death of the Writer?" *Salon*, September 23, 2023. https://www.salon.com/2023/09/23/are-we-witnessing-the-of-the-writer-facing-the-ai-crossroads-in-class-and-on-the-page/.

Saffron Huang, "ChatGPT and the Death of the Author," the *New Statesman*, February 26, 2023. https://www.newstatesman.com/the-weekend-essay/2023/02/chatgpt-death-author-big-tech-artificial-intelligence.

Abbie Klein, "ChatGPT: The End of Creative Writing?" *Tufts Daily*, April 5, 2023. https://www.tuftsdaily.com/article/2023/04/chatgpt-the-end-of-creative-writing.

John Lopez, "AI May Kill Us All, but It'll Never Write a Good Movie," *Vanity Fair*, July 11, 2023. https://www.vanityfair.com/hollywood/2023/07/ai-may-kill-us-all-but-itll-never-write-a-good-movie.

Alvin Powell, "Will ChatGPT Supplant Us as Writers, Thinkers?" *Harvard Gazette*, February 14, 2023. https://news.harvard.edu/gazette/story/2023/02/will-chatgpt-replace-human-writers-pinker-weighs-in/.

ChatGPT, AI, and the Future of Writing

Henry Williams, "I'm a Copywriter. I'm Pretty Sure Artificial Intelligence Is Going to Take My Job," the *Guardian*, January 24, 2023. https://www.theguardian.com/commentisfree/2023/jan/24/chatgpt-artificial-intelligence-jobs-economy.

Chapter 2

Will ChatGPT Benefit Student Writing?

Chapter Preface

Professional writers aren't the only people who are finding their lives upended by ChatGPT. The AI has also barged into the classroom, leaving students and teachers wondering whether or not to use this technology. If they do choose to use it, what's the most ethical and effective way to do so? It's a complicated issue, and one that can't be answered by simply saying, "Yes, go ahead and use ChatGPT. Everything will be fine!" or "Don't you dare use ChatGPT for schoolwork or for teaching! No good can come of it!"

In this chapter, the authors venture into the territory between those two extremes. Can ChatGPT be used to do a better job of teaching and learning? If so, how? And if the AI is not useful in the classroom, how do we get it out? In addition, they discuss not only how ChatGPT is being used in the classroom now, but how it might be in the future.

Some of the writers here see ChatGPT as a threat to education because it makes it much easier for students to cheat. Others argue that students are already cheating. Solving *that* problem will require more than restricting technology, they say.

Others suggest using ChatGPT as a teaching tool. If used carefully, the program can, they say, help guide students in their writing and help teach them how to evaluate a piece of writing, their own or the chatbot's. Going beyond the issue of whether students are using AI to cheat (or will in the future), some authors look at whether AI is changing the way students think.

VIEWPOINT 1

> *"ChatGPT and its competitors are tools, hence not in and of themselves 'bad' or 'good.' Rather, they have potential to support learning through modeling of certain types of writing, providing prompts for discussion or creative works, and offering additional aid or perspective to students."*

ChatGPT Will Change the Classroom, for Good or Ill

Nicole Lazar, James Byrns, Danielle Crowe, Meghan McGinty, Angela Abraham, Mike Guo, Megan Mann, Prithvi Narayanan, Lydia Roberts, Benjamin Sidore, and Maxwell Wager

In this viewpoint, Nicole Lazar discusses the findings of a survey of teachers and students from a Pennsylvania high school on the impact of ChatGPT on education (the other authors of this viewpoint were students at this school). Both the students and teachers express a mix of optimism and concern about the role ChatGPT could have in high schools. Among the benefits discussed are ChatGPT's ability to create discussion questions and prompts for writing. It could also be beneficial in modeling certain types of writing for students, such as AP

"Perils and Opportunities of ChatGPT: A High School Perspective," by Nicole Lazar, James Byrns, Danielle Crowe, Meghan McGinty, Angela Abraham, Mike Guo, Megan Mann, Prithvi Narayanan, Lydia Roberts, Benjamin Sidore, and Maxwell Wager, Harvard Data Science Review, October 27, 2023, https://hdsr.mitpress.mit.edu/pub/1cbv006q/release/1. Licensed under CC BY 4.0 International.

essays. However, the potentially negative aspects of ChatGPT include increased risk of plagiarizing work and preventing students from learning how to craft essays themselves if they count on ChatGPT to create the initial draft. Overall, both groups acknowledge that ChatGPT is simply a tool—not good or bad—and that with proper guidance on how to use it, it can be beneficial for high school students and educators. Nicole Lazar is a professor and department head in the department of statistics at Penn State University. At the time this viewpoint was published, the other authors were students at State College Area High School in State College, Pennsylvania.

As you read, consider the following questions:

1. What benefits did teachers suggest ChatGPT could have in education? What benefits did students mention?
2. What potential issues did students mention about the information ChatGPT provides? Why do they think it's different from a search engine?
3. According to this viewpoint, how could ChatGPT be used in a way that doesn't violate academic integrity?

Since its introduction on November 30, 2022, OpenAI's ChatGPT has generated discussion in the popular and trade press. Much of this discussion has focused on the ways in which ChatGPT and other artificial intelligence (AI) algorithms are disrupting education, writing, and creating, especially at the university level and in business. More overlooked has been another group whose education and careers will be affected by advances in generative artificial intelligence: high school students and their teachers.

To learn about the concerns and expectations of this group, in February 2023 one of us (Lazar) contacted her local high school, State College Area High School in State College, Pennsylvania. She recruited teachers and students who were willing to share their thoughts and current understanding on a variety of questions.

Once the volunteers were found, documents created in Google Docs were shared separately with the teachers and the students, allowing each set to answer independently. Over the course of a week and half, the participants had the opportunity to respond to the questions, as well as to react to the comments of their peers, a collaborative style of work to which all were accustomed. In this way, we obtained a quick snapshot of the opinions of a small—and not necessarily representative—group of high school students and teachers. We stress that the goal was to get a "pulse" in order to gauge how one slice of the high school population viewed these new technologies as they were starting to become readily available.

Three teachers—an English teacher, a computer science teacher, and a media arts teacher—provided their responses. Seven students, all 11th graders (16 or 17 years old) at State College Area High School at the initial stage of recruitment in spring 2023 also participated. In what follows, we summarize the themes that arose from the two discussions. This is not meant to be formal research, but rather a collection of our opinions and ideas. We differentiate between the thoughts of teachers and students primarily where they diverge.

We also note here that ChatGPT and its ilk are large language models, a type of sophisticated machine learning algorithm. These algorithms "learn" from training data—in this case, gleaned from the internet. The definition of (generative) artificial intelligence is somewhat fuzzier, but in popular discourse around these technologies, they are commonly called AI. We use AI and generative AI interchangeably in the rest of the discussion.

We all saw ways in which ChatGPT and similar AI chatbots could be supportive of learning. Teachers mentioned a variety of avenues by which ChatGPT might bring benefits to their students. For example, they thought that it could help support discussion, critical thinking, and collaboration in the classroom or spark ideas for students who may be stuck on a creative assignment. Specific benefits discussed included ChatGPT as a "rubber duck debugger" that can talk back; using a ChatGPT-generated solution as the starting point for further conversation; and brainstorming to show a variety of perspectives on a topic. Other positive uses proposed by the teachers were to model writing for certain types of assignments, to be an extra team member for students looking to push themselves beyond the scope of a class, and to fulfill a tutoring role. For example, if a student had difficulty with some idea or concept when teachers were not readily available (e.g. on the weekend), consulting with ChatGPT could clarify the issue, allowing the student to proceed. We would point out, however, that ChatGPT has been shown to "hallucinate" or make up answers when none are readily available and even in situations where they are (e.g. making up biographical information or research references). Students need to be made aware of this possibility and need to keep in mind that follow-up research will often be necessary.

Students echoed many of these same potential benefits. They saw ChatGPT as a resource to understand topics that they may struggle with in class and to further their knowledge acquisition by going beyond the class content. Also as noted by students, ChatGPT can simplify the process of looking for information, allowing them to spend more time on analysis and synthesis. Some other positive uses that students identified included generating email outlines, simplifying complex questions, and summarizing articles. Like the teachers, students thought that ChatGPT could be helpful as a tutor when they get stuck—for example, if studying for a test, they can get an answer quickly rather than having to wait for a teacher to reply to an email. In addition, ChatGPT could give a different perspective on concepts learned in class. Furthermore, students, like teachers, saw a role for the technology in brainstorming, as a first step in the creative process.

Students also considered the use of these technologies from a social and academic support perspective. For example, many students in the United States take Advanced Placement (AP) courses which, if they do well on the accompanying AP tests, can earn them college credit. Open-ended essay questions on the AP tests in subjects like English and history, such as the rhetorical analysis essay and the long essay question, often have a required structure and format. ChatGPT is adept at composing responses that match these structures and formats, which can be helpful for students with limited access to study guides and other preparatory resources. As also mentioned by one of the teachers, ChatGPT can provide a model for students on how to engage in certain types of writing.

On the other hand, a significant fear surrounding these technologies, as expressed in the trade press, is the threat posed to academic integrity. Indeed, not long after ChatGPT was introduced, people and companies were already at work on counter-technologies that could recognize when a paper had been written using AI. Notably, these tools themselves are not always accurate, since some writing styles may be more prone to (incorrect) identification as having been machine generated. Certain types of formulaic writing may also be flagged by AI detectors, since both the generators and the detectors rely on probabilities of word combinations. It is thus not surprising that we pointed to issues around cheating as a major peril. We thought, however, that the situation was more nuanced than the simple "use of ChatGPT is cheating" assertion. Respondents from both groups mentioned that context matters, and that AI could be used ethically. Proper citation, for example, was seen as crucial. Students and teachers alike strongly stated that students need to acknowledge when they use these tools in their work. Similarly, copying responses directly was rightly considered to be plagiarism, whether from a ChatGPT-generated response or any other resource that students might have access to.

Students raised a variety of other concerns as well. Several students noted that ChatGPT is not truly a search engine and should not be treated or used as one. It can return false information or make things up. Clearly, if students do not understand that and use it as a pure research tool, they can be misled. The students were skeptical of the credibility of the algorithms and thought that, like with Wikipedia, other sources should be consulted to verify results

ChatGPT, AI, and the Future of Writing

returned by ChatGPT. This requires awareness about the limitations of the technology and guidance on how to use it effectively.

Another point raised by the students related to how overreliance on tools like ChatGPT could be actively harmful. If students do not learn how to write on their own, instead taking the "shortcut" of an AI-generated essay, this could be detrimental to them in the long run when they get to university or to a job. They also reported that the use of existing shortcuts, including math-generating tools such as Mathway and Photomath, is already prevalent. Hence, ChatGPT could contribute further to the decline of independent learning. Finally, when students have not learned or analyzed the material on their own, classroom discussions suffer; they will not have developed their own perspectives and ideas to share, leading to a poorer experience for the class as a whole.

A final cluster of perceived disadvantages from the student perspective had to do with worries about misalignments between teacher expectations and results that might be returned by ChatGPT. This took the form of teachers perhaps looking for a particular interpretation of a text or math and science formulas gleaned from online sources that might not correspond to the process that teachers want students to follow.

Both groups shared other concerns and expectations around ChatGPT and the role it—and other large language models—will possibly play in their future lives and careers.

Teachers indicated that they would be looking to industry, academia, and professional societies for guidance on how to use ChatGPT and similar systems, what standards they should implement, and how to craft policies around acceptable and unacceptable use. All three teachers thought that ChatGPT is not, in and of itself, bad or good; rather, it is a technological tool like many others. As tools, chatbots hold promise to enhance education, but at this early point, it is still too soon to know if that promise will be fulfilled or not.

Students also considered ChatGPT to be a tool like any other, with both advantages and disadvantages. Several of the students argued that schools should teach them how to use AI ethically, since it is going to be a part of their lives. Students should understand how to adapt to changes in technology, since technology plays a key role in many aspects of modern society and is not static. In a similar vein, students thought that schools should not just ignore the issue or ban tools outright, but rather should think about how these tools can complement the educational experience. This will be part of the world the students will live and work in and they need to learn how to use these tools well.

Some students thought it was important to note that these algorithms have biases, since they are trained on data available online and generated by humans. Students need to know that generative AI tools could contain these biases as well, and hence need to be cautious of the results they return—that is, not to take them at face value. Other students wanted to know if ChatGPT might feed users false notions and provide justification for inaccurate information if asked certain questions in certain ways.

Though the group represented here is self-selected, we think that a number of important ideas are raised by the discussion. ChatGPT and its competitors are tools, hence not in and of themselves "bad" or "good." Rather, they have potential to support learning through modeling of certain types of writing, providing prompts for discussion or creative works, and offering additional aid or perspective to students. On the other hand, students and teachers alike are leery of the potential drawbacks to these technologies— diminishing the ability of students to think for themselves, enabling plagiarism, perpetuating biases, and providing false information.

Teachers and students are looking for guidance on how to navigate these technologies successfully, while being aware of the fact that the landscape is definitely not static. As if to prove this point, while we were writing this article in March 2023, OpenAI rolled out a new and improved algorithm: GPT-4. In the ensuing months, as we went through the publication process, the technologies and their uses continued to shift. But no doubt the same issues persist. Students would like schools to help them learn

ChatGPT, AI, and the Future of Writing

how to use AI algorithms ethically, rather than outright banning technologies that will continue to be part of their educational and professional lives. Teachers, in turn, are looking for help in understanding the benefits and limitations of ChatGPT, GPT-4, and the like. The educational system at the high school level, not just higher education, will have much to grapple with as these technologies continue to evolve.

References

Chomsky, N. (2023, March 8). The false promise of ChatGPT. *The New York Times*. https://www.nytimes.com/2023/03/08/opinion/noam-chomsky-chatgpt-ai.html

Chrisinger, B. (2023, February 22). It's not just our students – ChatGPT is coming for faculty writing. *The Chronicle of Higher Education*. https://www.chronicle.com/article/its-not-just-our-students-ai-is-coming-for-faculty-writing

Knight, W. (2023, March 9). Yes, ChatGPT is coming for your office job. *WIRED*. https://www.wired.com/story/yes-chatgpt-is-coming-for-your-office-job/

McMurtrie, B. (2022, December 13). AI and the future of undergraduate writing. *The Chronicle of Higher Education*. https://www.chronicle.com/article/ai-and-the-future-of-undergraduate-writing

Surovell, E. (2023, February 8) ChatGPT has everyone freaking out about cheating. It's not the first time. *The Chronicle of Higher Education*. https://www.chronicle.com/article/chatgpt-has-everyone-freaking-out-about-cheating-its-not-the-first-time

VIEWPOINT

> *"The sophistication and capability of AI technologies are accelerating. Rather than reacting with trepidation, we must find and embrace the positives."*

We Should Use AI to Change the Way We Assess Students' Work

Sam Illingworth

In the previous viewpoint the authors explored how students and teachers might use ChatGPT to help students write better and perform better academically. Here, Sam Illingworth suggests a completely different approach: turn the tables, and let students critique the work of the AI. This would make it difficult for students to plagiarize, help them develop their critical thinking and feedback skills, and ultimately enable them to develop skills more relevant to their future careers. Alternatively, Illingworth suggests that ChatGPT could be beneficial in developing prompts and exercises specifically related to students' professional interests, thus also helping them prepare for their future careers. Sam Illingworth is an associate professor in the department of learning and teaching enhancement at Edinburgh Napier University, Scotland.

"ChatGPT: students could use AI to cheat, but it's a chance to rethink assessment altogether" by Sam Illingworth, The Conversation, January 19, 2023, https://theconversation.com/chatgpt-students-could-use-ai-to-cheat-but-its-a-chance-to-rethink-assessment-altogether-198019. Licensed under CC BY-ND 4.0 International.

ChatGPT, AI, and the Future of Writing

As you read, consider the following questions:

1. What problems might occur if ChatGPT is used to grade students' writing assignments?
2. What problems does Illingworth see with the way assignments are assessed currently?
3. Were you surprised to learn that the first four paragraphs of this essay were written by ChatGPT?

ChatGPT is a powerful language model developed by OpenAI that has the ability to generate human-like text, making it capable of engaging in natural language conversations. This technology has the potential to revolutionize the way we interact with computers, and it has already begun to be integrated into various industries.

However, the implementation of ChatGPT in the field of higher education in the UK poses a number of challenges that must be carefully considered. If ChatGPT is used to grade assignments or exams, there is the possibility that it could be biased against certain groups of students.

For example, ChatGPT may be more likely to give higher grades to students who write in a style that it is more familiar with, potentially leading to unfair grading practices. Additionally, if ChatGPT is used to replace human instructors, it could perpetuate existing inequalities in the education system, such as the under-representation of certain demographics in certain fields of study.

There is also the potential for ChatGPT to be used to cheat on exams or assignments. Since it is able to generate human-like text, ChatGPT could be used to write entire assignments or essays, making it difficult for educators to detect cheating.

For example, ChatGPT (meaning "generative pre-trained transformer") could be asked to "write an essay about the challenges that ChatGPT poses higher education in the UK." In fact, the first four paragraphs of this article were written by ChatGPT, in response to this exact request.

| 54

ChatGPT's response (and this is your human author writing now) actually amounted to more than four paragraphs, as it went on to articulate its inability to fully replicate the expertise and real-world experience that human teachers bring to the classroom. This particular line of enquiry made me both appreciative of its concern for my job security, and somewhat cynical of its Machiavellian designs to win me over.

In my research and teaching, I am involved in developing assessment and feedback processes that enrich the student experience, while also equipping them with the skills they need upon graduation.

The truth is, if I was looking at 200 pieces of work submitted by first-year undergraduate students on this topic, I would probably give ChatGPT's efforts a pass. But far from being worried about the challenges this AI programme might pose, I see this instead as an opportunity to improve the way we assess learning in higher education.

Finding Opportunities

For me, the major challenge that ChatGPT presents is one I should be considering anyway: how can I make my assessments more authentic—meaning, useful and relevant. Authentic assessments are designed to measure students' knowledge and skills in a way that is particularly tailored to their own lives and future careers.

These assessments often involve tasks or activities that closely mirror the challenges students may encounter in real life, requiring them to apply knowledge and skills in a practical or problem-solving context. Specific examples might include asking a group of engineering students to collaborate on a community issue as part of the Engineers without Borders challenge, or inviting environmental science students to curate an art exhibition in a local gallery that explores the local impact of the climate crisis.

While there will always be a need for essays and written assignments—especially in the humanities, where they are essential to help students develop a critical voice—do we really need all

ChatGPT, AI, and the Future of Writing

ChatGPT Is Making It Easier to Cheat

The artificial intelligence software known as ChatGPT is disrupting so many industries.

The AI was developed by a company called Open AI. While some are praising the technology, others are raising ethical concerns, especially regarding education.

"You're not learning if the software is doing it for you," said Alexander Davidson, an English teacher at the University of Detroit Jesuit High School.

Davidson said writing and communication are two of the most important skills students can learn in their high school years. However, he fears a new technology can make that more difficult and students caught using it could get in big trouble.

"It will count as plagiarism because it's not their original thought, a computer wrote it for them," he said.

The computer that Davidson is referring to is ChatGPT. The "GPT" stands for generative pre-trained transformer and the software can do just about anything you ask it to do, like write English essays.

Right now, it's nearly impossible for educators to know students are using it and that is pretty scary, according to Davidson.

"If there is no way to track it, do we even bother with an essay anymore?" Davidson said.

students to be writing the same essays and responding to the same questions? Could we instead give them autonomy and agency and in doing so, help to make their assessments more interesting, inclusive and ultimately authentic?

As educators, we can even use ChatGPT directly to help us develop such assessments. So, rather than posing the question that generated the start of this article, I could instead present students with ChatGPT's response alongside some marking instructions, and ask them to provide a critique on what grade the automated response deserves and why.

Will ChatGPT Benefit Student Writing?

At the college level, some educators are taking a slightly different approach to ChatGPT.

"I think it's a useful tool," said Christopher Susak, an English professor at Wayne State University. "We started playing with it as soon as it became public, immediately we started talking about redesigning a curriculum we were already using as an opportunity to incorporate it into the classroom," Susak added.

Susak and Dr. Jared Grogan said they both believe it's necessary to teach students how to use ChatGPT, but there are still some concerns.

"I think it's a little scary for students," Grogan said.

Grogan said students have some anxiety about the need to learn new technologies so quickly and this is no exception.

"Things are moving really fast for them, they're really interested in it, I think they feel there is a need to master it to some extent," Grogan said.

Susak said he too has some reservations about the technology.

"At least now as it stands, it cannot determine what is a truth and what is a lie when it is feeding a recommendation to someone," Susak said.

Open AI recently announced it is releasing a tool to help educators detect whether or not Chat GPT was used to write essays.

"I am hopeful we get these tools by next year," said Davidson.

"ChatGPT making it easier for students to cheat in school," by Gino Vicci. CBS Broadcasting Inc., February 28, 2023.

Such an assessment would be much more difficult to plagiarize. It would also invite the students to develop their critical thinking and feedback skills, both of which are essential when they graduate into the workforce, no matter what their profession. Alternatively, ChatGPT could be used to generate scenario-based tasks that require students to analyze and solve problems they may encounter in their future careers.

This feels like a Pandora's box moment for assessment in higher education. Whether we decide to embrace ChatGPT in our pursuit of authentic assessment or passively acknowledge the

ChatGPT, AI, and the Future of Writing

ethical dilemmas it might present to academic integrity, there is a real opportunity here. This could help us reflect on how we assess our students and why this might need to change. Or, in the AI's own words:

ChatGPT could be a useful tool for creating authentic assessments, but it would still be up to the instructor to design and implement the assessment in a way that is meaningful and relevant for their students.

The sophistication and capability of AI technologies are accelerating. Rather than reacting with trepidation, we must find and embrace the positives. Doing so will help us think about how we can specifically tailor the assessment of students, and provide better and more creative support for their learning.

VIEWPOINT 3

> *"Along with addressing the deeper reasons why students cheat, we need to teach students how to understand and think critically about this technology."*

ChatGPT Isn't Increasing Cheating

Carrie Spector

The introduction of ChatGPT has caused many educators to worry that students will use the AI to cheat. In this viewpoint, Carrie Spector interviews two scholars who have researched cheating in school: Denise Pope, a senior lecturer at Stanford Graduate School of Education (GSE), and Victor Lee, an associate professor at GSE. They are not, for the most part, worried that ChatGPT and its ilk will cause students to cheat more than they already are. According to their research, cheating already happens at relatively high rates and ChatGPT simply is a new tool for doing that. In order to address this issue, educators must tackle the factors that cause students to cheat, not potential tools for doing so. Carrie Spector is a senior communications associate at Stanford University.

As you read, consider the following questions:

1. Why are the researchers interviewed here confident that the students they surveyed are being honest in their responses?

"What do AI chatbots really mean for students and cheating?" by Carrie Spector. Stanford University, October 31, 2023. Reprinted with permission.

ChatGPT, AI, and the Future of Writing

2. Why, according to these scholars, do students cheat?
3. What advice do the people interviewed here offer educators?

The launch of ChatGPT and other artificial intelligence (AI) chatbots has triggered an alarm for many educators, who worry about students using the technology to cheat by passing its writing off as their own. But two Stanford researchers say that concern is misdirected, based on their ongoing research into cheating among U.S. high school students before and after the release of ChatGPT.

"There's been a ton of media coverage about AI making it easier and more likely for students to cheat," said Denise Pope, a senior lecturer at Stanford Graduate School of Education (GSE). "But we haven't seen that bear out in our data so far. And we know from our research that when students do cheat, it's typically for reasons that have very little to do with their access to technology."

Pope is a co-founder of Challenge Success, a school reform nonprofit affiliated with the GSE, which conducts research into the student experience, including students' well-being and sense of belonging, academic integrity, and their engagement with learning. She is the author of *Doing School: How We Are Creating a Generation of Stressed-Out, Materialistic, and Miseducated Students,* and coauthor of *Overloaded and Underprepared: Strategies for Stronger Schools and Healthy, Successful Kids.*

Victor Lee is an associate professor at the GSE whose focus includes researching and designing learning experiences for K–12 data science education and AI literacy. He is the faculty lead for the AI + Education initiative at the Stanford Accelerator for Learning and director of CRAFT (Classroom-Ready Resources about AI for Teaching), a program that provides free resources to help teach AI literacy to high school students.

Here, Lee and Pope discuss the state of cheating in U.S. schools, what research shows about why students cheat, and their recommendations for educators working to address the problem.

What do we know about how much students cheat?

Pope: We know that cheating rates have been high for a long time. At Challenge Success we've been running surveys and focus groups at schools for over 15 years, asking students about different aspects of their lives—the amount of sleep they get, homework pressure, extracurricular activities, family expectations, things like that—and also several questions about different forms of cheating.

For years, long before ChatGPT hit the scene, some 60 to 70 percent of students have reported engaging in at least one "cheating" behavior during the previous month. That percentage has stayed about the same or even decreased slightly in our 2023 surveys, when we added questions specific to new AI technologies, like ChatGPT, and how students are using it for school assignments.

Isn't it possible that they're lying about cheating?

Pope: Because these surveys are anonymous, students are surprisingly honest—especially when they know we're doing these surveys to help improve their school experience. We often follow up our surveys with focus groups where the students tell us that those numbers seem accurate. If anything, they're underreporting the frequency of these behaviors.

Lee: The surveys are also carefully written so they don't ask, point-blank, "Do you cheat?" They ask about specific actions that are classified as cheating, like whether they have copied material word for word for an assignment in the past month or knowingly looked at someone else's answer during a test. With AI, most of the fear is that the chatbot will write the paper for the student. But there isn't evidence of an increase in that.

So AI isn't changing how often students cheat—just the tools that they're using?

ChatGPT, AI, and the Future of Writing

Lee: The most prudent thing to say right now is that the data suggest, perhaps to the surprise of many people, that AI is not increasing the frequency of cheating. This may change as students become increasingly familiar with the technology, and we'll continue to study it and see if and how this changes.

But I think it's important to point out that, in Challenge Success' most recent survey, students were also asked if and how they felt an AI chatbot like ChatGPT should be allowed for school-related tasks. Many said they thought it should be acceptable for "starter" purposes, like explaining a new concept or generating ideas for a paper. But the vast majority said that using a chatbot to write an entire paper should never be allowed. So this idea that students who've never cheated before are going to suddenly run amok and have AI write all of their papers appears unfounded.

But clearly a lot of students are cheating in the first place. Isn't that a problem?

Pope: There are so many reasons why students cheat. They might be struggling with the material and unable to get the help they need. Maybe they have too much homework and not enough time to do it. Or maybe assignments feel like pointless busywork. Many students tell us they're overwhelmed by the pressure to achieve— they know cheating is wrong, but they don't want to let their family down by bringing home a low grade.

We know from our research that cheating is generally a symptom of a deeper, systemic problem. When students feel respected and valued, they're more likely to engage in learning and act with integrity. They're less likely to cheat when they feel a sense of belonging and connection at school, and when they find purpose and meaning in their classes. Strategies to help students feel more engaged and valued are likely to be more effective than taking a hard line on AI, especially since we know AI is here to stay and can actually be a great tool to promote deeper engagement with learning.

What would you suggest to school leaders who are concerned about students using AI chatbots?

Pope: Even before ChatGPT, we could never be sure whether kids were getting help from a parent or tutor or another source on their assignments, and this was not considered cheating. Kids in our focus groups are wondering why they can't use ChatGPT as another resource to help them write their papers—not to write the whole thing word for word, but to get the kind of help a parent or tutor would offer. We need to help students and educators find ways to discuss the ethics of using this technology and when it is and isn't useful for student learning.

Lee: There's a lot of fear about students using this technology. Schools have considered putting significant amounts of money in AI-detection software, which studies show can be highly unreliable. Some districts have tried blocking AI chatbots from school wifi and devices, then repealed those bans because they were ineffective.

AI is not going away. Along with addressing the deeper reasons why students cheat, we need to teach students how to understand and think critically about this technology. For starters, at Stanford we've begun developing free resources to help teachers bring these topics into the classroom as it relates to different subject areas. We know that teachers don't have time to introduce a whole new class, but we have been working with teachers to make sure these are activities and lessons that can fit with what they're already covering in the time they have available.

I think of AI literacy as being akin to driver's ed: We've got a powerful tool that can be a great asset, but it can also be dangerous. We want students to learn how to use it responsibly.

VIEWPOINT 4

> *"If AI text generation does our writing for us, we diminish opportunities to think out problems for ourselves."*

By Taking Over Our Writing, AI-Driven Programs Rob Us of the Ability to Think

Naomi S. Baron

Naomi Baron is a linguist who studies the role of technology in writing and reading. In this viewpoint, she argues that ChatGPT is just the latest development in decades of AI that undermine the way we write, and by extension, our ability to think. Spellcheck, Grammarly, predictive texting, and autocompleted online searches are all other examples of ways in which AI has made writing and researching easier in the recent past. AI-driven programs—including but not limited to ChatGPT—have the potential for preventing students from developing a writing style and critical thinking skills. Naomi Baron is a professor emerita at American University.

As you read, consider the following questions:

1. What AI-driven editing tools does Baron say have already affected our writing?
2. How can AI undermine the writer's voice?

"How ChatGPT robs students of motivation to write and think for themselves" by Naomi S. Baron, https://theconversation.com/how-chatgpt-robs-students-of-motivation-to-write-and-think-for-themselves-197875. The Conversation, January 19, 2023. Licensed under CC BY-ND 4.0 International.

3. How can writing aids such as ChatGPT hinder our thinking, according to Baron and several writers she cites here?

When the company OpenAI launched its new artificial intelligence program, ChatGPT, in late 2022, educators began to worry. ChatGPT could generate text that seemed like a human wrote it. How could teachers detect whether students were using language generated by an AI chatbot to cheat on a writing assignment?

As a linguist who studies the effects of technology on how people read, write and think, I believe there are other, equally pressing concerns besides cheating. These include whether AI, more generally, threatens student writing skills, the value of writing as a process, and the importance of seeing writing as a vehicle for thinking.

As part of the research for my new book on the effects of artificial intelligence on human writing, I surveyed young adults in the U.S. and Europe about a host of issues related to those effects. They reported a litany of concerns about how AI tools can undermine what they do as writers. However, as I note in my book, these concerns have been a long time in the making.

Users See Negative Effects

Tools like ChatGPT are only the latest in a progression of AI programs for editing or generating text. In fact, the potential for AI undermining both writing skills and motivation to do your own composing has been decades in the making.

Spellcheck and now sophisticated grammar and style programs like Grammarly and Microsoft Editor are among the most widely known AI-driven editing tools. Besides correcting spelling and punctuation, they identify grammar issues as well as offer alternative wording.

65 |

ChatGPT, AI, and the Future of Writing

AI text-generation developments have included autocomplete for online searches and predictive texting. Enter "Was Rome" into a Google search and you're given a list of choices like "Was Rome built in a day." Type "ple" into a text message and you're offered "please" and "plenty." These tools inject themselves into our writing endeavors without being invited, incessantly asking us to follow their suggestions.

Young adults in my surveys appreciated AI assistance with spelling and word completion, but they also spoke of negative effects. One survey participant said that "At some point, if you depend on a predictive text [program], you're going to lose your spelling abilities." Another observed that "Spellcheck and AI software ... can ... be used by people who want to take an easier way out."

One respondent mentioned laziness when relying on predictive texting: "It's OK when I am feeling particularly lazy."

Personal Expression Diminished

AI tools can also affect a person's writing voice. One person in my survey said that with predictive texting, "[I] don't feel I wrote it."

A high school student in Britain echoed the same concern about individual writing style when describing Grammarly: "Grammarly can remove students' artistic voice. ... Rather than using their own unique style when writing, Grammarly can strip that away from students by suggesting severe changes to their work."

In a similar vein, Evan Selinger, a philosopher, worried that predictive texting reduces the power of writing as a form of mental activity and personal expression.

"[B]y encouraging us not to think too deeply about our words, predictive technology may subtly change how we interact with each other," Selinger wrote. "[W]e give others more algorithm and less of ourselves. ... [A]utomation ... can stop us thinking."

In literate societies, writing has long been recognized as a way to help people think. Many people have quoted author Flannery O'Connor's comment that "I write because I don't know what

I think until I read what I say." A host of other accomplished writers, from William Faulkner to Joan Didion, have also voiced this sentiment. If AI text generation does our writing for us, we diminish opportunities to think out problems for ourselves.

One eerie consequence of using programs like ChatGPT to generate language is that the text is grammatically perfect. A finished product. It turns out that lack of errors is a sign that AI, not a human, probably wrote the words, since even accomplished writers and editors make mistakes. Human writing is a process. We question what we originally wrote, we rewrite, or sometimes start over entirely.

Challenges in Schools

When undertaking school writing assignments, ideally there is ongoing dialogue between teacher and student: Discuss what the student wants to write about. Share and comment on initial drafts. Then it's time for the student to rethink and revise. But this practice often doesn't happen. Most teachers don't have time to fill a collaborative editorial—and educational—role. Moreover, they might lack interest or the necessary skills, or both.

Conscientious students sometimes undertake aspects of the process themselves—as professional authors typically do. But the temptation to lean on editing and text generation tools like Grammarly and ChatGPT makes it all too easy for people to substitute ready-made technology results for opportunities to think and learn.

Educators are brainstorming how to make good use of AI writing technology. Some point up AI's potential to kick-start thinking or to collaborate. Before the appearance of ChatGPT, an earlier version of the same underlying program, GPT-3, was licensed by commercial ventures such as Sudowrite. Users can enter a phrase or sentence and then ask the software to fill in more words, potentially stimulating the human writer's creative juices.

ChatGPT, AI, and the Future of Writing

A Fading Sense of Ownership

Yet there's a slippery slope between collaboration and encroachment. Writer Jennifer Lepp admits that as she increasingly relied on Sudowrite, the resulting text "didn't feel like mine anymore. It was very uncomfortable to look back over what I wrote and not really feel connected to the words or ideas."

Students are even less likely than seasoned writers to recognize where to draw the line between a writing assist and letting an AI text generator take over their content and style.

As the technology becomes more powerful and pervasive, I expect schools will strive to teach students about generative AI's pros and cons. However, the lure of efficiency can make it hard to resist relying on AI to polish a writing assignment or do much of the writing for you. Spellcheck, grammar check and autocomplete programs have already paved the way.

Writing as a Human Process

I asked ChatGPT whether it was a threat to humans' motivation to write. The bot's response:

"There will always be a demand for creative, original content that requires the unique perspective and insight of a human writer."

It continued: "[W]riting serves many purposes beyond just the creation of content, such as self-expression, communication, and personal growth, which can continue to motivate people to write even if certain types of writing can be automated."

I was heartened to find the program seemingly acknowledged its own limitations.

My hope is that educators and students will as well. The purpose of making writing assignments must be more than submitting work for a grade. Crafting written work should be a journey, not just a destination.

VIEWPOINT 5

> *"Of course high-school English is not dead. Of course writing and creativity remain the province of human agents. The fact that such questions can even be asked reveals that we have, as a culture, long misunderstood the nature of the liberal arts and even intelligence itself."*

Those Who Worry About ChatGPT Ruining Writing Exercises in Schools Miss the Point of Writing

Walker Larson

In this viewpoint, Walker Larson discusses recent arguments that ChatGPT will completely change and undermine the teaching of writing. Some, such as the author of a piece Larson discusses in this viewpoint, argue that academic writing may not even be a suitable metric of intelligence and learning if it can be generated by AI. However, though Larson acknowledges that it may be harder to detect cheating on papers now, to make this kind of argument misses the point of writing. He argues that the purpose of writing is functioning as a kind of thought process and the communication of these thoughts. It plays an important role in helping students learn to think for this reason. Even with the rise of AI, writing will still have

"What Is Writing? Why We Misunderstand the Coming of ChatGPT," by Walker Larson, Intellectual Takeout, January 23, 2023, https://intellectualtakeout.org/2023/01/writing-the-coming-of-chatgpt/. Licensed under CC BY-SA 4.0 International.

69 |

ChatGPT, AI, and the Future of Writing

a place in education for students who want to learn how to think and communicate their thoughts. Walker Larson teaches literature at a private academy in Wisconsin and is the author of two novels.

As you read, consider the following questions:

1. What does Larson mean when he says that, as a teacher, he is more concerned with "purpose, intention, and process" than the end product?
2. According to Larson, why do programs like ChatGPT not produce a "message" in their writing?
3. What does Larson believe is wrong about the way we view language and writing, and what does he blame for this shift in opinion?

Is high-school English dead?

A Dec. 9 article published in *The Atlantic* by Daniel Herman, a high-school English teacher, says yes. Herman asserts that the new AI chat program ChatGPT drastically changes the nature of education, especially the teaching of writing. The software can respond to prompts of almost any kind—even very complicated ones—in a convincing human-like manner.

Specifically, Herman questions whether academic writing remains a relevant and teachable skill—or even a fitting metric for intelligence—now that ChatGPT can autogenerate essays that are better than most student writing. And education isn't the only area that may be impacted by the program's impressive abilities. The concern is that any industry, task, or job involving writing could be affected.

Certainly, ChatGPT comes to us as a force to be reckoned with. It will be harder to detect cheating, for example, and information online must be treated with even more skepticism. But this sudden outburst of concern over the future of education and other intellectual pursuits because "the computer can do it better" makes little sense.

| 70

These cries of dismay could only come from a society that has lost track of what intelligence, thought, creativity, and writing really are.

Let's take the field of education, for example. "It's no longer obvious to me that my teenagers actually will need to develop this basic skill [of writing]," writes Herman. Toward the end of the essay, he asks a fatal question:

> Many teachers have reacted to ChatGPT by imagining how to give writing assignments now—maybe they should be written out by hand, or given only in class—but that seems to me shortsighted. The question isn't 'How will we get around this?' but rather 'Is this still worth doing?'

These words are tinged with a note of despair: what's the point, anymore? Computers have finally overtaken us in the realm of abstract thinking, writing, and art, just like they did in mathematics, chess, and scientific modelling.

Like Herman, I am a high-school English teacher, but questions like these never even cross my mind in connection with AI chatbots. In my teaching, I am not looking only at *outcome* or *end product*, but at *purpose, intention,* and *process.*

Of course high-school English is not dead. Of course writing and creativity remain the province of human agents. The fact that such questions can even be asked reveals that we have, as a culture, long misunderstood the nature of the liberal arts and even intelligence itself.

We are dealing with a denial of the soul and free will, a failure to distinguish between man and machine. Herman doubts the usefulness of his profession because we can get the same or better end product using AI as we can get when we teach kids how to write on their own. So why teach writing? This scientific, output-oriented approach looks at the two end products—one written by a human being, the other by a computer—and compares them as though they are comparable. But in reality, they bear no similarity because the agents and processes are completely different.

Writing encompasses a thought process and a communication. One reason to write is that writing helps us learn how to think even as we share those thoughts with others. Writing is a message with

ChatGPT, AI, and the Future of Writing

a meaning. But in order for there to be meaning in something, someone must put it there—a conscious, rational mind, using its free will, must put sense and intention into the message.

That meaning is then extracted by another conscious, free mind. What the computer produces is not actually a message by that definition. In a very real sense, the computer's "essay" is meaningless because there is no conscious intent behind it by a rational, self-aware mind. There was only a complex, lifeless algorithm of some sort created by a team of programmers. It *simulates* a communication, a message, but it is just another one of those simulations that plague our modern world and try to deprive us of the real thing. There is nothing real behind it.

The computer has no intentions behind its messages because, lacking a soul and a conscious mind, it has no intentions at all. It has been "trained" by scanning countless texts written by real people and "learned" the patterns of our language—patterns used by those who are actually communicating.

The computer just blindly apes this process by using statistics to predict what kind of word should go where, based off the millions of model messages it has "read." But it does not know what they *mean*. So when we talk to chatbots like this, we are not really communicating: we are only hearing an echo of our own, human thoughts, a kind of reconstruction of fragmented sentences from the millions of sentences by real people swirling around on the internet. These are our *own* words.

As far as actual education is concerned, such a tool is useless. Using ChatGPT to "write" for you does not teach you thinking or communication. And it's absurd to equate an AI-generated text, however seemingly eloquent, with something written by an actual student. In the case of the student, actual thinking and communication (however fuzzy) happens. In the other case, only a convincing illusion of communication occurs.

Perhaps the ills connected with ChatGPT are our punishment for forgetting what we used to know about language. In 1967, Roland Barthes wrote an essay called "The Death of the Author"

| 72

that called into question traditional literary interpretation and, indeed, the nature of communication in general. Barthes argued that we can't rely upon the intention or biography of an author to find the "ultimate meaning" of a text. We can never know what intention or objective meaning lies behind a message. For Barthes, there is no "ultimate meaning" because the meaning of a text is created by the reader, not the author. And the author—like Victor Frankenstein—vanishes and dies, overcome by the Thing he has created, which takes on an autonomous life. Meaning escapes from the hand of the author and, at best, is recreated in hundreds of mutated ways by the reader. In such a scenario, true communication becomes impossible.

We can thank ideas like death of the author for corrupting our understanding of what writing is. These ideas prepared the way for us to view a computer-generated text and a human-generated text on the same plane. Since we have denied the relevance and even existence of a rational intention behind communication, what difference does it make if the message comes from man or machine?

Drawing upon the nihilism found in the Eastern philosophy he teaches, Herman expresses this despairing relativism succinctly in the conclusion of his essay:

> Everything is made up; it's true. The essay as a literary form? Made up. Grammatical rules as markers of intelligence? Writing itself as a technology? Made up. Starting now, OpenAI is forcing us to ask foundational questions about whether any of those things are worth keeping around.

But, of course, for those of us who believe that meaning can and must exist in language and communication as a product of intelligent and free minds, it remains essential to keep writing. If we hope to think well and deeply, and share our thoughts and our hearts with other intelligent, conscious beings, then we must keep teaching and learning to write. In a society that equates man and machine as well as matter and spirit, the art of writing—*true, human* writing, messy, disorderly, but carrying all the heft and blaze of actual human thought and feeling—is needed now more than ever.

VIEWPOINT 6

| "In writing courses, students can begin to see the critical variety and power of one of our best technologies: the human act of writing, a system of finite resources but infinite combinations."

The Rise of AI Makes Learning to Write More Important than Ever Before

Joel Heng Hartse and Taylor Morphett

In this viewpoint, Joel Heng Hartse and Taylor Morphett discuss the role of undergraduate writing courses at universities, which have come under fire with the rise of generative AI. Some argue that because AI can handle the fundamentals of writing, such as grammar, it isn't necessary for students to take these courses. However, the authors assert that these classes do not (or should not) just teach the mechanics of writing—they should also teach students to engage intellectually with topics and communicate that in writing. The problem, according to the authors, is that universities do not currently invest enough resources into developing strong writing courses, and that this has been an issue since before generative AI entered the discussion. Joel Heng Hartse is a senior lecturer in the faculty of education at Simon Fraser University in British Columbia,

"Writing Is a Technology that Restructures Thought—and In an AI Age, Universities Need to Teach It More," by Joel Heng Hartse and Taylor Morphett, The Conversation, February 26, 2024, https://theconversation.com/writing-is-a-technology-that-restructures-thought-and-in-an-ai-age-universities-need-to-teach-it-more-219482. Licensed under CC BY-ND 4.0 International.

Canada. Taylor Morphett is an instructor of English at Kwantlen Polytechnic University in British Columbia.

As you read, consider the following questions:

1. According to the authors, what is technology?
2. Why do the authors assert that AI does not produce "good writing"?
3. According to this viewpoint, what tasks do students perform in writing that cannot be performed by AI?

In an age of AI-assisted writing, is it important for university students to learn how to write?

We believe it is now more than ever.

In the writing classroom, students get the time and help they need to understand writing as not only a skill, but what the language scholar Walter J. Ong called a "technology that restructures thought."

"Technology" is not simply iPhones or spreadsheets—it is about mediating our relationship with the world through the creation of tools, and writing itself is arguably the most important tool for thinking that university students need to master.

Perhaps not surprisingly, not everyone agrees.

Role of University Writing Courses

"Eliminate the Required First-Year Writing Course" was the headline of a provocative article published in *Inside Higher Ed* in November.

In this article, a professor of writing studies, Melissa Nicolas of Washington State University, writes that while she has seen reason to question how efficient first-year composition courses are before now, "the advent of generative artificial intelligence is the final nail in the coffin."

In her estimation, "learning to write and writing to learn are two distinct things." First-year writing courses are "largely about learning to write, but AI can now do this for us. Writing to learn is much more complicated and is something that can only be done by the human mind."

We take issue with this distinction. From the perspective of human learning and development, the grammatically correct prose produced by generative AI like ChatGPT is not "good writing"—even if it is or seems factually correct—if it does not reflect intellectual engagement with its subject matter. This is not to mention serious questions about the meaning of gaining insight from digital data, issues surrounding data biases, and so on.

First-year composition and other writing courses are a crucial part of the way university students are socialized into ways of communicating that will benefit them far beyond their undergraduate years.

Canadian Versus American Universities

We propose another solution to the problem Nicolas raises of first-year composition courses being formulaic and outdated. Universities need to devote resources to expanding and improving writing programs, including first-year composition.

We especially need this in Canada, where, as doctoral research carried out by one of the authors of this piece (Taylor Morphett) has shown, first-year composition has traditionally been under-emphasized, and writing has only been taught in a piecemeal way.

When first-year composition courses began to develop at the end of the 19th century in the United States, in Canada the focus was on the fine-tuning of literary taste and the reading of canonical British literature.

The philosophies of education and approaches to teaching that developed from this early time are still present today in Canada. Writing education is often seen by universities as a remedial skill, something students should already know how to do.

In reality, much more writing instruction is needed. Today's undergraduates are plunged into a sea of texts, information and technology they have immense difficulty navigating, and ChatGPT has made it harder, not easier, for students to discern the credibility of sources.

Writing Programs in Canada

In writing courses, students can begin to see the critical variety and power of one of our best technologies: the human act of writing, a system of finite resources but infinite combinations. They learn to think, synthesize, judge the credibility of sources and information and interact with an audience—none of which can be done by AI.

Thankfully, some universities have taken the lead in making writing a cornerstone of undergraduate education. For example, the University of Victoria has a robust academic writing requirement for all students, regardless of their field of study. At the University of Toronto Mississauga, first-year students take an innovative for-credit writing course that takes a "writing-about-writing" approach. In this program, undergraduates study writing as an academic subject itself, not just a skill. They learn about the importance, complexity and socially situated nature of academic writing.

Needed at All Universities

All Canadian universities should make a beginning academic writing or communication course required for all undergraduates, along with discipline-specific upper-division writing courses focused on scholarly and professional genres in their fields.

Academic and professional writing is a second language for everyone: no one is born knowing how to properly cite sources or craft airtight business proposals.

We need dedicated writing programs to help students understand and communicate complex concepts to a specific audience for a specific purpose in rhetorically flexible ways, with an awareness of their responsibilities to a human community of readers.

ChatGPT, AI, and the Future of Writing

Skills and Knowledge to Make a Difference

Generative AI like ChatGPT cannot do this, because it cannot know or "understand" anything. Its *raison d'être* is to produce plausible strings of symbols in response to human prompts, based on data it has been trained upon.

We have knowledgeable and talented PhDs graduating in communication, applied linguistics, English, rhetoric and related fields whose expertise in these areas is sorely needed at institutions across the country.

If Canada wants to graduate domestic and international students with the skills and knowledge to make a difference in the world, we need to be training them in writing.

Periodical and Internet Sources Bibliography

The following articles have been selected to supplement the diverse views presented in this chapter.

Abreanna Blose, "As ChatGPT Enters the Classroom, Teachers Weigh Pros and Cons," *NEA Today*, April 12, 2023. https://www.nea.org/nea-today/all-news-articles/chatgpt-enters-classroom-teachers-weigh-pros-and-cons.

Lauren Coffey, "Universities Build Their Own ChatGPT-like Tools," *Inside Higher Ed*, March 21, 2024. https://www.insidehighered.com/news/tech-innovation/artificial-intelligence/2024/03/21/universities-build-their-own-chatgpt-ai.

Daniel De Visé and Lexi Lonas, "ChatGPT Sends Shockwaves Across College Campuses," the *Hill,* March 19, 2023. https://thehill.com/homenews/education/3905672-chatgpt-sends-shockwaves-across-college-campuses/.

James R. Hagerty, "Is It OK for Students to Use ChatGPT? More Teachers Say Yes," the *Wall Street Journal*, November 5, 2023. https://www.wsj.com/tech/ai/teachers-ai-classroom-schools-678d7d84.

Will Douglas Heaven, "ChatGPT Is Going to Change Education, Not Destroy It," *MIT Technology Review*, April 6, 2023. https://www.technologyreview.com/2023/04/06/1071059/chatgpt-change-not-destroy-education-openai/.

Kayla Jimenez, "ChatGPT in the Classroom: Here's What Teachers and Students Are Saying," *USA Today*, March 1, 2023. https://www.usatoday.com/story/news/education/2023/03/01/what-teachers-students-saying-ai-chatgpt-use-classrooms/11340040002/.

Owen Kichizo Terry, "I'm a Student. You Have No Idea How Much We're Using ChatGPT," the *Chronicle of Higher Education*, May 12, 2023. https://www.chronicle.com/article/im-a-student-you-have-no-idea-how-much-were-using-chatgpt.

ChatGPT, AI, and the Future of Writing

Beth McMurtrie and Beckie Supiano, "ChatGPT Has Changed Teaching. Our Readers Tell Us How," *Chronicle of Higher Education*, December 11, 2023. https://www.chronicle.com/article/chatgpt-has-changed-teaching-our-readers-told-us-how.

Kevin Roose, "Don't Ban ChatGPT in Schools. Teach With It." the *New York Times*, January 12, 2023. https://www.nytimes.com/2023/01/12/technology/chatgpt-schools-teachers.html.

Olivia B. Waxman, "The Creative Ways Teachers Are Using ChatGPT in the Classroom," *Time*, August 8, 2023. https://time.com/6300950/ai-schools-chatgpt-teachers/.

CHAPTER 3

Will ChatGPT Help or Harm Journalists and Journalism?

Chapter Preface

In the first chapter of this volume, the authors looked at the potential effects of ChatGPT on writers of all kinds. They specifically addressed the question of whether or not this new technology would put writers out of work. The authors here focus specifically on journalists and the practice of journalism. They explore how ChatGPT might influence the practice and product of journalism. For example, does the tendency of AI to get facts wrong and even make things up preclude its use in a profession that is committed not only to telling the truth, but to finding the truth?

You might think that the answer is a resounding yes. But the authors here point out that it's not that simple. The role of ChatGPT in journalism does not have to include reporting—which is the stage where journalists find and verify facts. It can play a role in organizing material, deciding where to look for facts, and, in the end, writing up the story. All of this can (and must) be supervised by humans.

In any case, the current corporate model of journalism is that the people who pay the bills make the rules, and those people aren't journalists. That often puts serious journalists in the uncomfortable position of having to work with AI whether they like it or not. It's up to the humans in this partnership to make sure ChatGPT does no harm.

In this chapter, the authors look at the benefits and risks of AI in journalism, noting that for all its pitfalls, if used carefully, it can be useful. Of course, those pitfalls are deep, and require extreme caution on the part of the human in the partnership.

Another problem discussed here is that the use of ChatGPT can seriously damage the credibility of new organizations, and their credibility was already suffering. Fake news was already a hot button issue, and the use of ChatGPT in journalism may only make that worse.

But the chapter gets started with a close look by experts at the risks and benefits of AI in the newsroom, providing an overview of the common arguments for and against using AI in journalism.

VIEWPOINT 1

> *"ChatGPT will not answer a question by saying it does not know the answer; instead, if the data it has doesn't provide an answer, it will simply make one up."*

ChatGPT for Journalists: Both Useful and Risky

Marina Cemaj Hochstein

Jenna Burrell is the director of research at the nonprofit research organization Data & Society. In this viewpoint, Marina Cemai Hochstein writes about Burrell's ideas about the potential benefits and pitfalls of AI for journalists. She asserts that it can help simplify concepts in a way that is understandable for general audiences and that it may be useful in coming up with interview questions, but that the results it generates may not be accurate. Despite the potential issues, Burrell believes that how AI will impact journalism will become clearer as it becomes more widely used. Marina Cemaj Hochstein is a senior engagement associate at J Street, a nonprofit advocacy group dedicated to promoting American leadership to end the Arab–Israeli and Israeli–Palestinian conflicts.

"The benefits and pitfalls of ChatGPT for journalists" by Marina Cemaj Hochstein. International Center for Journalists, February 3, 2023. Reprinted with permission.

84

As you read, consider the following questions:

1. In what way might ChatGPT help journalists who aren't native speakers of English, according to Burrell?
2. What does Burrell see as the major flaw of ChatGPT?
3. What does ChatGPT do when asked a question it cannot find an answer for?

ChatGPT, an artificial intelligence (AI) language model created by OpenAI, has been making waves across the internet, leading to questions on how AI will change the way we work and write.

In the latest ICFJ Pamela Howard Forum on Global Crisis Reporting webinar, Jenna Burrell, director of research at Data & Society, dove into the pros of ChatGPT and how it can be a tool for journalists, as well as its limitations and what journalists should be cautious about.

Here are her tips on best uses of ChatGPT for journalists:

ChatGPT Can Simplify Concepts

One of the most important tasks for journalists is simplifying complex topics for a general audience. ChatGPT makes this easier, Burrell said. Using the language model allows journalists to plug an abstract or part of an academic article into ChatGPT and ask the software to simplify it. A journalist can use this tool to better understand an article or idea before interviewing the piece's author.

ChatGPT is also useful for non-native English speakers. Its simplification feature allows non-native English speakers who might be able to understand basic English to "translate" any work into a more basic form. This is especially useful for topics that use complex or specialized language like science or economics. For now, this only works in English.

It Can Assist You with Questions for Interviews

Journalists can use ChatGPT to prepare for interviews. You can list questions you have in mind for an interview subject, and the software will create more questions modeled after them. The software can also copy a previous interview, or an article written by the interviewee, and develop questions about that topic.

ChatGPT can be used as a copy-editor. Journalists can input their articles for a last review before sending them to their editor, for example by asking ChatGPT to edit the article in a specific format like AP style. However, journalists should still review and fact-check the changes ChatGPT makes to ensure that no information added is false.

You Cannot Always Trust Its Results

Journalists should be aware of ChatGPT's major flaw: it cannot be trusted. ChatGPT was trained on data found on the internet as of 2021, and it responds to prompts by making predictions on the most likely answer to queries. By using this model, it sometimes generates an answer that's not factually correct.

For example, when Burrell asked ChatGPT for experts in the field of data science, it produced a list of well-known academics who study the subject. However, when the question was modified to ask for Ghanaian experts in data science, none of the names it presented actually existed when checked.

Burrell warned journalists to be aware of ChatGPT's proclivity to "fill the data void." ChatGPT will not answer a question by saying it does not know the answer; instead, if the data it has doesn't provide an answer, it will simply make one up. This can be especially problematic in regions where the internet has been historically devoid of data. "Because it takes a little bit from here and there, it often produces just absolutely incorrect results and it's hard to figure out when it's incorrect," Burrell said.

ChatGPT also has an issue of replicating the bias it was built on. The software was built using a large amount of data, but the tool cannot "learn"—it can only reproduce and regurgitate the data it already has.

Because ChatGPT was built by collecting massive amounts of information from the internet, the information it gives back will be as biased as the information it was trained on. When journalists use ChatGPT, they should not only double-check the content it presents, but also reach out to others who have different perspectives, including those who might counter ChatGPT's built-in bias.

"ChatGPT sucks up everything on the internet; what you get out of it is a reflection of the skew of the internet as a whole," Burrell said.

The Future of ChatGPT in Journalism

ChatGPT is still a new tool, and questions remain on how its parent company, Open AI, will shape its business model. It is not yet clear how OpenAI will make money, whether or not it will partner with Microsoft and its search engine, Bing, or if it will create its own advertising model like those that Google and Bing currently use. While the tool is currently free (with a paid premium version recently announced) and open for everyone, any change in monetization might raise further questions regarding copyright law. For example, although ChatGPT was trained on every article journalists have written, the authors are not compensated or recognized for their contribution.

Burrell notes that this might be a bigger problem with tools like DALL-E, another Open AI tool, which creates images from text. Today, artists who make their lives from the art they create are seeing their styles copied by DALL-E with no credit or compensation. "Everything you've written as a journalist that's out there publicly is dumped into OpenAI's tool," Burrell said. "You have this copyrighted work that you've published as a journalist that informs that model, and you don't get compensated for that. I don't think copyright law is really up to the task at this moment."

ChatGPT, AI, and the Future of Writing

In the form ChatGPT exists today, Burrell recommended that journalists use it as a tool while recognizing its limitations. Although the model can help journalists write faster when they are on a deadline, inspire them when they are having trouble being creative, and serve as an extra step to ensure their work is well-written and stylized, it should always be used with a human by its side. Everything it says must still be double-checked for accuracy and for sources.

For journalists worrying that ChatGPT's writing will be passed off as journalism, Burrell notes that its writing lacks a level of journalistic quality and creativity—an editor can usually tell the difference. "Humans will continue to be much more inventive and creative, and able to produce really unusual ways of saying things," she said.

VIEWPOINT

| *"Outlets that use AI to put out as much content as possible are also part of the problem."*

AI Is Creating a Trust Problem for Media Outlets

Héloïse Hakimi Le Grand

In this viewpoint, Héloïse Hakimi Le Grand covers the highlights of a three-day conference on the responsible use of AI in journalism. One of the key issues discussed at the meeting was how to use AI while maintaining the trust of readers. Those in attendance generally agreed that AI can be a useful tool for journalists in helping them access and sort through data and attend to their audience's needs, but they should be wary of AI-generated content and make sure it does not spread misinformation. Héloïse Hakimi Le Grand is the communications and marketing manager at International Center for Journalists.

As you read, consider the following questions:

1. What are consumers of news and "content" looking for, according to one of the speakers at this event?
2. How might automation actually *help* news outlets spend more on intensive, time-consuming stories?

"How to Use Artificial Intelligence in Journalism Without Losing Audience Trust" by Héloïse Hakimi Le Grand. International Center for Journalists, July 14, 2023. Reprinted with permission.

ChatGPT, AI, and the Future of Writing

3. How can AI help journalists access data more easily, according to speakers mentioned here?

A t Media Party Chicago, a conference exploring the intersection of artificial intelligence and journalism, attendees debated and learned about the opportunities and dangers of AI. Ethics experts proposed frameworks for responsible use of powerful new technologies, developers taught journalists how to use AI to bring customized content to their readers and reporters wrestled with how to maintain audiences' trust while AI-aided disinformation abounds.

The International Center for Journalists (ICFJ) helped organize the three-day event, bringing together entrepreneurs, journalists, developers and designers from five continents to work together on the future of media. They all joined to devise solutions using AI at a hackathon.

Here are some of the key takeaways from the event:

What Questions Should Newsrooms Ask Themselves Before Using AI?

In a discussion with ICFJ's Senior Director of Innovation Maggie Farley, Dalia Hashim of Partnership on AI presented questions newsrooms should ask themselves before even starting to use generative artificial intelligence, the AI system capable of generating text and images in response to prompts. Communicating how and why you're using AI, Hashim said, is also important for building trust with audiences. "The more open and transparent you are about it, the more ready the audience is to accept that [AI] is being used," she explained. Important considerations include:

- Are we comfortable with using generative AI tools that were trained using others' content without consent? Can we find or make tools that are not derivative?

| 90

- How are we going to put guardrails around the use of AI tools in the newsroom?
- Where could our workflow be automated? Where do we need a human in the loop?
- If we are using AI to produce content, how will we label it?
- How will we ensure the accuracy of AI-aided content?
- If we're collecting data from the audiences, how is it going to be used and who owns it?

Hashim urged journalists to use the Partnership on AI's framework on responsible practices for newsrooms' AI use, alongside their AI tools database for local newsrooms.

How Can We Prevent AI from Spreading Disinformation? Is AI Hallucinating?

Edward Tian of GPT Zero highlighted some of the dangers of AI when it comes to dis/misinformation.

"AI generative text is prone to spitting out articles and hallucinating bouts," he reminded the audience.

He recommended that newsrooms be conscious of that as they're integrating AI technology into their work. It's not just ChatGPT that's spreading misinformation, he said. Outlets that use AI to put out as much content as possible are also part of the problem. Tian presented a free detection tool his company created to detect the use of AI. Newsrooms and audiences can use this tool to limit the spread of AI-driven misinformation, he explained.

What Can AI Do for Audiences?

Jeremy Gilbert of the Knight Lab at Northwestern University said that "all too often, we spend time asking, 'What can generative AI do?' but we don't ask, 'What does our audience actually want?'" Gilbert explained that news consumers don't necessarily want more content. Instead, they have specific questions that made them seek out a story, and the news outlet should be giving them specific

ChatGPT, AI, and the Future of Writing

LARGE LANGUAGE MODELS ARE AS BIASED AS THEIR TRAINING DATA

In her book, *Automated (Un)Intelligence,* data journalism professor Meridith Broussard explains that the term machine learning is somewhat misleading on its own. When computer scientists say that AI applications "learn," they don't quite mean learning in the human sense. AI learns from training data—large datasets that teach it statistical patterns in the world. Basically, the AI learns how to solve problems better and faster because it can predict what will happen from the data it learns from. The result of this however, is that the machine misses out on a lot of the nuances of human intelligence and communication—for example, it likely won't be able to detect sarcasm or figures of speech.

Additionally, AI is created by humans—and humans have bias. So if a dataset reflects human biases, the AI will produce a biased output. So, for example, when Amazon used AI to screen resumes and filter job applicants, it was quickly discovered that the algorithm was sorting out the resumes of women.

The algorithm was trained on the resumes of successful employees and Silicon Valley isn't known for its gender diversity. So, the application started rejecting resumes with feminine language in it, penalizing resumes that had the word "women" in it and resumes that contained the name of certain women's colleges. The result was that Amazon had to stop using the application shortly after introducing it.

[. . .]

"Nia Springer-Norris/Understand algorithmic bias in journalism" by Curators of the University of Missouri, November 21, 2022.

answers. Generative AI, he said, can help newsrooms build tools that better respond to the audience's needs.

Is AI Going to Replace Journalists?

World News Media Network CEO Martha Williams delved into the pros and cons of generative AI.

People are already starting to use ChatGPT to get information directly instead of from news outlets—or even Google. That means that advertising and subscriptions will suffer, Williams said. Disinformation will also increase. The challenge for media is to create unique, trusted content that is valuable to their communities—and their own AI tools to power it.

"I do believe anything that can be automated will be, and that's not just journalism. It's media jobs in general," she said. But Williams also said that automation could open up time and money to pursue more resource-intensive, large-scale journalism projects. Hearken's Jennifer Brandel made a similar point, explaining that in the future AI might be able to replace transactional jobs and create efficiencies in others. If AI can replace some of what journalists are doing, she said, we need to be doing something more human: creating connections with people and giving them the information they need to make lives and communities better.

Can AI Improve How Journalists Work?

Fernanda Aguirre of Mexico and Rosario Marina of Argentina presented a project they collaborated on after meeting each other through the ICFJ-run Emerging Media Leaders fellowship. To bypass the difficult-to-access-and-analyze data provided by the Argentinian judiciary, Aguirre created an AI tool for Marina's newsroom to use.

The tool turns PDF data into an easily readable format and then allows journalists to interview the data through the tool. "Of course, we've got limitations, generative AI is not perfect," said Aguirre. To combat those pitfalls, Aguirre and Marina include fact-checking prompts when interrogating the data, to ensure that all the information they're getting is actually coming from the original documents.

"There are a lot of stories journalists aren't finding because of unfriendly data formats," Aguirre said. AI tools like this one can now help journalists access datasets to create stories that keep the government accountable and communities informed.

ChatGPT, AI, and the Future of Writing

What Can Journalists Do that AI Can't?

In her keynote session, Jennifer Brandel of Hearken focused on the value what she calls "actual experience" (or AE) can bring to journalism.

"We have a 521 million-year-old technology called the human brain, which needs equal amounts of investment so it can optimize for things like care, compassion, deep listening, fully embodied information gathering, co-creation and dissemination," she said.

"We humans still have a competitive advantage when it comes to one dimension against AI, that is care," she said. "AI couldn't care less. It cannot intrinsically care. So journalists or those doing acts of journalism need to make up for what's lost, and care more."

On the final day of Media Party, journalists, developers, designers, and more got together for a Hackathon. Seven teams presented their ideas centered around the opportunities and challenges of AI in journalism. The following teams won awards from the Knight Lab and GPTZero and future mentoring from ICFJ:

- SourceScout, a platform that uses AI to help media outlets find diverse and under-recognized sources, won the top prize.
- The second prize went to Scroll News, a tool for news organizations to create social media-style news posts and short videos to engage young readers.
- Share a Story, a tool developed by journalism professor Blake Eskin to engage students in news selection and production tied for third prize.
- Quick Trace, a chatGPT-aided tool to help reporters parse large amounts of reported material, also received third prize.

VIEWPOINT 3

> *"In many schools across the U.S., teachers use outdated methods in identifying sketchy websites. . . . These methods are mostly useless when it comes to AI-generated, plausible false news organizations."*

AI Can Create Entire Fake News Sites, and That's a Huge Problem

Alex Mahadevan

So far in this chapter, the authors have been looking at the use of ChatGPT in and by journalists at existing news sources. In this viewpoint, Alex Mahadevan looks at the problem of fake news sites created entirely by ChatGPT. There are many imperfections in these sites—at least for now—but experts consider this a troubling trend in part because AI is able to create news sites that look real, lending them an air of authenticity and reliability that they do not possess. Alex Mahadevan is director of MediaWise, the Poynter Institute's digital media literacy project that teaches people of all ages how to spot misinformation online.

As you read, consider the following questions:

1. What is "pink slime"?

"This newspaper doesn't exist: How ChatGPT can launch fake news sites in minutes" by Alex Mahadevan. Poynter Institute, February 3, 2023. Reprinted with permission.

ChatGPT, AI, and the Future of Writing

2. Why is the advice students are given for vetting websites no longer as useful as it once was?

3. How are some news sites complicit in this problem, according to Mahadevan?

Michael Martinez, managing editor of the *Suncoast Sentinel*, is a foodie who loves jazz, volunteers at local homeless shelters and spends his days hiking in Florida's state parks.

One problem: Neither Martinez, nor the *Suncoast Sentinel*, exist.

In less than a half hour, and with just a few sentences of input, the buzzy AI text-generator ChatGPT spit out details about Martinez—that he's worked in journalism for 15 years and "has a reputation for being a strong leader and excellent mentor"— and a masthead of reporters, editors and a photographer for the nonexistent *Suncoast Sentinel*.

"Okay I am freaked out," tweeted former White House official Tim Wu—who coined the term net neutrality in 2003—when I posted my first attempt at made-up newspapers with ChatGPT.

I'm always skeptical about tech freak-outs. But, in just a few hours, anyone with minimal coding ability and an ax to grind could launch networks of false local news sites—with plausible-but-fake news items, staff and editorial policies—using ChatGPT.

Here's how it works, from my colleague Seth Smalley:

"The technology works by sifting through the internet, accessing vast quantities of information, processing it, and using artificial intelligence to generate new content from user prompts. Users can ask it to produce almost any kind of text-based content."

Political operatives, lobbyists and ad dollar-chasing grifters have launched dubious news sites—referred to as "pink slime"—in relatively short order without using a tool like ChatGPT. Some hired contractors in the Philippines to produce stories, while others used algorithms—the foundation of AI—to generate hundreds of articles based on government databases, said Priyanjana Bengani,

| 96

senior research fellow at the Tow Center at Columbia Journalism School, who studies pink slime networks.

"Are the barriers to entry getting lower? The answer is yes," Bengani said. "Now anybody sitting anywhere can spin one of these things up."

In about two minutes, while juggling other tasks, I used thispersondoesnotexist.com—another AI tool — to generate headshots for Martinez, editor-in-chief Sarah Johnson, copy editor Sarah Nguyen, photographer Jennifer Davis, and others.

"Shining a light on St. Petersburg" was ChatGPT's first crack at a slogan for the *Suncoast Sentinel*. It spit out "Uncovering the stories that matter in St. Petersburg" when I asked for something a little more exciting.

It wrote me editorial and corrections policies, a couple letters to the editor, and totally fabricated articles about a new local art gallery and BusinessBoost, a fake app developed by fake St. Petersburg entrepreneurs.

It generated an article accusing local officials of rigging the election. And an article alleging the mayor ran a no-bid scheme in one of the biggest redevelopment projects in the area's history.

I even asked ChatGPT to generate the HTML code for the homepage of the burgeoning fake newspaper and it complied. And it gave me a starting point for more complex Javascript code to make the fake site "sexy and interactive."

Its results weren't flawless. It got the name of the mayor wrong twice (there have been a few elections since Rick Baker was in office, bot). And, as you can see with Martinez's bio, ChatGPT generates ridiculously boring copy.

"I don't think it's going to be transformative overnight," said Bengani, noting that the media (yes, me included) also freaked out about deepfakes two years ago and DALL-E last year. We've yet to see impactful disinformation campaigns materialize from either—the highly publicized deepfake of Ukrainian President Volodymyr Zelenskyy was quickly debunked.

ChatGPT, AI, and the Future of Writing

The model doesn't update in real time, and can't provide specific details that the locals who would be affected by an issue would look for in a story (for example, ChatGPT wouldn't provide the size or cost of the redevelopment project I used in my experiment).

Going back to the false business story I created, you can see the cracks in ChatGPT that would make an editor cringe—or tear their hair out. Here's a paragraph from the "story":

> The founders of the company, brothers Tom and Jerry Lee, were inspired to create the app after seeing the struggles of small business owners in the St. Petersburg area. They saw a need for an affordable and accessible solution that would help these business owners compete in today's fast-paced business environment.
>
> "Small business owners are the backbone of our local economy," said Tom Lee. "We wanted to create a tool that would help them succeed, and that's exactly what BusinessBoost does."

It reads like a student skimmed the pages of *The Wall Street Journal* for business buzzwords and regurgitated them out with a couple of fake names and a hilariously ill-conceived business. But that is kind of how ChatGPT works, right?

To defend against ChatGPT's potential use as a tool for misinformation, among other malicious uses, OpenAI has already launched a "classifer" to identify AI-generated text. I laughed out loud when I plugged in some chunks of this experiment and received:

"The classifier considers the text to be possibly AI-generated." OK.

Still, as director of Poynter's digital media literacy initiative MediaWise, I know that most people judge a "news" website based on how legitimate it looks, including its bylines and web design.

That may have been at least a semi-reliable measure in the past, but with ChatGPT, for example, it's simple to launch a false news site that satisfies all of those "signals."

"Previously a well written, well laid out publication with headshots and bylines, etc., meant something," said Mike Caulfield, a research scientist at the University of Washington's Center for an

Informed Public who teaches media literacy tactics, in a Twitter message. "It didn't always mean it was reputable, but there was at least a partial correlation between something looking that way and being known, or 'real'—even if 'real' and wrong. Signals of authority were expensive, and that formed a barrier to entry."

In many schools across the U.S., teachers use outdated methods in identifying sketchy websites, said Caulfield, who has an upcoming book with Stanford History Education Group founder Sam Wineburg that includes a chapter on this issue. These methods are mostly useless when it comes to AI-generated, plausible false news organizations.

"What has happened over the past 30 years is that the formerly expensive signals—the ones that focused on surface features—have become incredibly cheap," he said. "But we are still teaching students to look for those signals. It's a massive disaster in the making."

Lateral reading, one of the foundational media literacy techniques developed by SHEG and taught by MediaWise, encourages users to leave a website and use a search engine to find out more about the news outlet or other organization instead of relying on the website's "about us" page or masthead, for example.

Bengani suggests copying and pasting text from a potential pink slime website into Google to look for plagiarism—a major red flag in identifying these networks.

OpenAI didn't respond to a request for comment, but when I asked ChatGPT about how AI like itself could impact the information ecosystem, it replied:

"Generated content can easily spread misinformation, especially if it is not thoroughly fact-checked or if it is generated with biased or inaccurate data. Additionally, the ease with which AI can generate large volumes of content can make it difficult for users to determine the credibility of a source. This can make it easier for false or misleading information to spread, potentially undermining public trust in journalism and information as a whole.

It's important for AI models like me to be used responsibly and in accordance with ethical guidelines, such as providing balanced

ChatGPT, AI, and the Future of Writing

and fair reporting and protecting the privacy and dignity of sources and subjects. Additionally, it's important for news organizations to fact-check and verify all information before publishing it, whether it was generated by AI or not."

ChatGPT's complicated relationship with journalism doesn't end with quick-scaling false news websites. Trusted news sites have already fumbled with AI and produced misinformed copy. CNET was recently caught doing it, and BuzzFeed said it will start using ChatGPT-based technology to generate "new forms of content."

"I think the problem is that it's not just what the pink slime guys are doing," Bengani said.

VIEWPOINT 4

> *"Many organizations were really concerned about not losing their credibility, not losing their audience, not trying to give away what makes journalism stand out—especially in a world where misinformation is around in a much larger scale than ever before."*

News Organizations Are Developing Policies to Maintain Journalistic Integrity While Using AI

Clark Merrefield

Since ChatGPT was launched in late 2022, many news organizations have had to grapple with how they believe AI should be used in journalism and which policies are necessary to preserve an organization's integrity while using the new tool. In this viewpoint, Clark Merrefield examines recent research on AI policies and guidelines that have been implemented at news organizations around the world. Many news organizations are concerned about how AI may threaten the accuracy of reporting and reveal confidential sources, and their guidelines caution journalists to take measures to counteract these potential issues. Many organizations also find it

"Researchers Compare AI Policies and Guidelines at 52 New Organizations Around the World," by Clark Merrefield, Journalist's Resource, Shorenstein Center on Media, Politics and Public Policy, Harvard Kennedy School, December 12, 2023, https://journalistsresource.org/home/generative-ai-policies-newsrooms/. Licensed under CC BY-ND 4.0 International.

101 |

ChatGPT, AI, and the Future of Writing

important to disclose when AI is used in a piece. Despite concerns, news organizations acknowledge that AI can be a useful tool for journalists as long as they proceed with care. Clark Merrefield is a senior editor of economics and legal systems at the Journalist's Resource at Harvard Kennedy School.

As you read, consider the following questions:

1. Which journalistic values are mentioned as being commonly cited in guidelines regarding the use of AI by news organizations?
2. How did the researchers compare AI policies and guidelines from various news organizations?
3. What does Nick Diakopoulos mean by hybridity when talking about the use of AI in newsrooms?

In July 2022, just a few newsrooms around the world had guidelines or policies for how their journalists and editors could use digital tools that run on artificial intelligence. One year later, dozens of influential, global newsrooms had formal documents related to the use of AI.

In between, artificial intelligence research firm OpenAI launched ChatGPT, a chatbot that can produce all sorts of written material when prompted: lines of code, plays, essays, jokes and news-style stories. Elon Musk and Sam Altman founded OpenAI in 2015, with multibillion dollar investments over the years from Microsoft.

Newsrooms including *USA Today, The Atlantic,* National Public Radio, the Canadian Broadcasting Corporation and the *Financial Times* have since developed AI guidelines or policies—a wave of recognition that AI chatbots could fundamentally change the way journalists do their work and how the public thinks about journalism.

| 102

Research posted during September 2023 on preprint server SocArXiv is among the first to examine how newsrooms are handling the proliferating capabilities of AI-based platforms. Preprints have not undergone formal peer review and have not been published in an academic journal, though the current paper is under review at a prominent international journal according to one of the authors, Kim Björn Becker, a lecturer at Trier University in Germany and a staff writer for the newspaper *Frankfurter Allgemeine Zeitung*.

The analysis provides a snapshot of the current state of AI policies and documents for 52 news organizations, including newsrooms in Brazil, India, North America, Scandinavia and Western Europe.

Notably, the authors write that AI policies and documents from commercial news organizations, compared with those that receive public funding, "seem to be more fine-grained and contain significantly more information on permitted and prohibited applications."

Commercial news organizations were also more apt to emphasize source protection, urging journalists to take caution when, for example, using AI tools for help making sense of large amounts of confidential or background information, "perhaps owing to the risk legal liability poses to their business model," they write.

Keep reading to learn what else the researchers found, including a strong focus on journalistic ethics across the documents, as well as real world examples of AI being used in newsrooms—plus, how the findings compare with other recent research.

AI Guidance and Rules Focus on Preserving Journalistic Values

AI chatbots are a type of generative AI, meaning they create content when prompted. They are based on large language models, which themselves are trained on huge amounts of existing text. (OpenAI

ChatGPT, AI, and the Future of Writing

rivals Google and Meta in the past year have announced their own large language models).

So, when you ask an AI chatbot to write a three-act play, in the style of 19th century Norwegian playwright Henrik Ibsen, about the struggle for human self-determination in a future dominated by robots, it is able to do this because it has processed Ibsen's work along with the corpus of science fiction about robots overtaking humanity.

Some news organizations for years have used generative AI for published stories, notably the Associated Press for simple coverage of earnings reports and college basketball game previews. Others that have dabbled in AI-generated content have come under scrutiny for publishing confusing or misleading information.

The authors of the recent preprint paper analyzed the AI policies and guidelines, most of them related to generative AI, to understand how publishers "address both expectations and concerns when it comes to using AI in the news," they write.

The most recent AI document in the dataset is from NPR, dated July 2023. The oldest is from the Council for Mass Media, a self-regulatory body of news organizations in Finland, dated January 2020.

"One thing that was remarkable to me is that the way in which organizations dealt with AI at this stage did exhibit a very strong sense of conserving journalistic values," says Becker. "Many organizations were really concerned about not losing their credibility, not losing their audience, not trying to give away what makes journalism stand out—especially in a world where misinformation is around in a much larger scale than ever before."

Other early adopters include the BBC and German broadcaster Bayerischer Rundfunk, "which have gained widespread attention through industry publications and conferences," and "have served as influential benchmarks for others," the authors write.

Many of the documents were guidelines—frameworks, or best practices for thinking about how journalists interact with and use AI, says Christopher Crum, a doctoral candidate at Oxford

University and another co-author. But a few were prescriptive policies, Crum says.

Among the findings:

- Just over 71% of the documents mention one or more journalistic values, such as public service, objectivity, autonomy, immediacy—meaning publishing or broadcasting news quickly—and ethics.
- Nearly 70% of the AI documents were designed for editorial staff, while most of the rest applied to an entire organization. This would include the business side, which might use AI for advertising or hiring purposes. One policy only applied to the business side.
- And 69% mentioned AI pitfalls, such as "hallucinations," the authors write, in which an AI system makes up facts.
- About 63% specified the guidelines would be updated at some point in the future—6% of those "specified a particular interval for updates," the authors write—while 37% did not indicate if or when the policies would be updated.
- Around 54% of the documents cautioned journalists to be careful to protect sources when using AI, with several addressing the potential risk of revealing confidential sources when feeding information into an AI chatbot.
- Some 44% allow journalists to use AI to gather information and develop story ideas, angles and outlines. Another 4% disallow this use, while half do not specify.
- Meanwhile, 42% allow journalists to use AI to alter editorial content, such as editing and updating stories, while 6% disallow this use and half do not specify.
- Only 8% state how the AI policies would be enforced, while the rest did not mention accountability mechanisms.

ChatGPT, AI, and the Future of Writing

How the Research Was Conducted

The authors found about two-thirds of the AI policy documents online and obtained the remainder through professional and personal contacts. About two-fifths were written in English. The authors translated the rest into English using DeepL, a translation service based on neural learning, a backbone of AI.

They then used statistical software to break the documents into five-word blocks, to assess their similarity. It's a standard way to linguistically compare texts, Crum says. He explains that the phrase "I see the dog run fast" would have two five-word blocks: "I see the dog run," and "see the dog run fast."

If one document said, "I see the dog run fast" while another said, "I see the dog run quickly," the first block of five words would be the same, the second block different—and the overall similarity between the documents would be lower than if the sentences were identical.

As a benchmark for comparison, the authors performed the same analysis on the news organizations' editorial guidelines. The editorial guidelines were a bit more similar than the AI guidelines, the authors find.

"Because of the additional uncertainty in the [AI] space, the finding is that the AI guidelines are coalescing at a slightly lower degree than existing editorial guidelines," Crum says. "The potential explanation might be, and this is speculative and not in the paper, something along the lines of, editorial guidelines have had more time to coalesce, whereas AI guidelines at this stage, while often influenced by existing AI guidelines, are still in the nascent stages of development."

The authors also manually identified overarching characteristics of the documents relating to journalistic ethics, transparency and human supervision of AI. About nine-tenths of the documents specified that if AI were used in a story or investigation, that had to be disclosed.

"My impression is not that organizations are afraid of AI," Becker says. "They encourage employees to experiment with this

| 106

new technology and try to make some good things out of it—for example, being faster in their reporting, being more accurate, if possible, finding new angles, stuff like that. But at the same time, indicating that, under no circumstances, shall they pose a risk on journalistic credibility."

AI in the Newsroom Is Evolving

The future of AI in the newsroom is taking shape, whether that means journalists primarily using AI as a tool in their work, or whether newsrooms become broadly comfortable with using AI to produce publicly facing content. The Journalist's Resource has used DALL•E 2, an OpenAI product, to create images to accompany human-reported and written research roundups and articles.

Journalists, editors and newsroom leaders should, "engage with these new tools, explore them and their potential, and learn how to pragmatically apply them in creating and delivering value to audiences," researcher and consultant David Caswell writes in a September 2023 report for the Reuters Institute for the Study of Journalism at Oxford. "There are no best practices, textbooks or shortcuts for this yet, only engaging, doing and learning until a viable way forward appears. Caution is advisable, but waiting for complete clarity is not."

The Associated Press in 2015 began using AI to generate stories on publicly traded firms' quarterly earnings reports. But recently, the organization's AI guidelines released during August 2023 specify that AI "cannot be used to create publishable content and images for the news service."

The AP had partnered with AI-content generation firm Automated Insights to produce the earnings stories, The Verge reported in January 2015. The AP also used Automated Insights to generate more than 5,000 previews for NCAA Division I men's basketball games during the 2018 season.

Early this year, *Futurism* staff writer Frank Landymore wrote that tech news outlet CNET had been publishing AI-generated articles. Over the summer, Axios' Tyler Buchanan reported *USA Today* was

ChatGPT, AI, and the Future of Writing

pausing its use of AI to create high school sports stories after several such articles in *The Columbus Dispatch* went viral for peculiar phrasing, such as "a close encounter of the athletic kind."

And on Nov. 27, Futurism published an article by Maggie Harrison citing anonymous sources alleging that *Sports Illustrated* has recently been using AI-generated content and authors, with AI-generated headshots, for articles on product reviews.

Senior media writer Tom Jones of the Poynter Institute wrote the next day that the "story has again unsettled journalists concerned about AI-created content, especially when you see a name such as *Sports Illustrated* involved."

The Arena Group, which publishes *Sports Illustrated*, posted a statement on X the same day the Futurism article was published, denying that *Sports Illustrated* had published AI-generated articles. According to the statement, the product review articles produced by a third-party company, AdVon Commerce, were "written and edited by humans," but "AdVon had writers use a pen or pseudo name in certain articles to protect author privacy— actions we strongly condemn—and we are removing the content while our internal investigation continues and have since ended the partnership."

On Dec. 11, the Arena Group fired its CEO. Arena's board of directors "met and took actions to improve the operational efficiency and revenue of the company," the company said in a brief statement, which did not mention the AI allegations. Several other high level Arena Group executives were also fired last week, including the COO, according to the statement.

Many of the 52 policies reviewed for the preprint paper take a measured approach. About half caution journalists against feeding unpublished work into AI chatbots. Many of those that did were from commercial organizations.

For example, reporters may obtain voluminous government documents, or have hundreds of pages of interview notes or transcripts and may want to use AI to help make sense of it all. At

| 108

least one policy advised reporters to treat anything that goes into an AI chatbot as published—and publicly accessible, Becker says.

Crum adds that the research team was "agnostic" in its approach—not for or against newsrooms using AI—with the goal of conveying the current landscape of newsroom AI guidelines and policies.

Themes on Human Oversight in Other Recent Research

In July, University of Amsterdam postdoctoral researcher Hannes Cools and Northwestern University communications professor Nick Diakopoulos published an article for the Generative AI in the Newsroom project, which Diakopoulos edits, examining publicly available AI guidelines from 21 newsrooms.

Cools and Diakopoulos read the documents and identified themes. The guidelines generally stress the need for human oversight. Cools and Diakopoulos examined AI documents from many of the same newsrooms as the preprint authors, including the CBC, Insider, Reuters, Nucleo, *Wired* and Mediahuis, among others.

"At least for the externally facing policies, I don't see them as enforceable policies," says Diakopoulos. "It's more like principal statements: 'Here's our goals as an organization.'"

As for feeding confidential material into AI chatbots, Diakopoulos says that the underlying issue is about potentially sharing that information with a third party—OpenAI, for example—not in using the chatbot itself. There are "versions of generative AI that run locally on your own computer or on your own server," and those should be unproblematic to use as a journalistic tool, he says.

"There was also what I call hybridity," Diakopoulos says. "Kind of the need to have humans and algorithms working together, hybridized into human-computer systems, in order to keep the quality of journalism high while also leveraging the capabilities of AI and automation and algorithms for making things more efficient or trying to improve the comprehensiveness of investigations."

ChatGPT, AI, and the Future of Writing

For local and regional newsrooms interested in developing their own guidelines, there may be little need to reinvent the wheel. The Paris Charter, developed among 16 organizations and initiated by Reporters Without Borders, is a good place to start for understanding the fundamental ethics of using AI in journalism, Diakopoulos says.

VIEWPOINT 5

> "Even if we believe that AI systems are a necessary part of the future for our society, it seems like a bad idea to destroy the sources of data that they were originally trained on."

Does OpenAI Have a Right to Use Data from Journalism to Train ChatGPT?

Mike Cook

In December 2023, the New York Times filed a lawsuit against ChatGPT's creator OpenAI for infringing on their copyright by using their journalism to train ChatGPT. In this viewpoint, Mike Cook explains that the New York Times argues that OpenAI has used their work to create a product that could compete with them and potentially put them out of business. OpenAI, however, argues that this is considered fair use of journalism because it transforms it into something new. OpenAI also claims that ChatGPT is intended to be a tool for journalists and writers, though many news organizations and creative writers don't buy this. Cook argues that the fair use laws that apply to humans should not apply to AI, as AI is not human and doesn't function the same way we do in remixing and transforming content. Mike Cook is a senior lecturer in the department of informatics at King's College London.

"The *New York Times*' Lawsuit Against OpenAI Could Have Major Implications for the Development of Machine Intelligence," by Mike Cook, The Conversation, January 10, 2024, https://theconversation.com/the-new-york-times-lawsuit-against-openai-could-have-major-implications-for-the-development-of-machine-intelligence-220547. Licensed under CC BY-ND 4.0 International.

ChatGPT, AI, and the Future of Writing

As you read, consider the following questions:

1. What do advocates of AI mean when they say AI "learns" from data?
2. What evidence does Cook provide suggesting that AI systems do store training data?
3. Why does Cook believe fair use laws as they currently exist should not apply to AI?

In 1954, the *Guardian*'s science correspondent reported on "electronic brains", which had a form of memory that could let them retrieve information, like airline seat allocations, in a matter of seconds.

Nowadays the idea of computers storing information is so commonplace that we don't even think about what words like "memory" really mean. Back in the 1950s, however, this language was new to most people, and the idea of an "electronic brain" was heavy with possibility.

In 2024, your microwave has more computing power than anything that was called a brain in the 1950s, but the world of artificial intelligence is posing fresh challenges for language— and lawyers. Last month, the *New York Times* newspaper filed a lawsuit against OpenAI and Microsoft, the owners of popular AI-based text-generation tool ChatGPT, over their alleged use of the *Times*' articles in the data they use to train (improve) and test their systems.

They claim that OpenAI has infringed copyright by using their journalism as part of the process of creating ChatGPT. In doing so, the lawsuit claims, they have created a competing product that threatens their business. OpenAI's response so far has been very cautious, but a key tenet outlined in a statement released by the company is that their use of online data falls under the principle known as "fair use". This is because, OpenAI argues, they transform the work into something new in the process—the text generated by ChatGPT.

| 112

At the crux of this issue is the question of data use. What data do companies like OpenAI have a right to use, and what do concepts like "transform" really mean in these contexts? Questions like this, surrounding the data we train AI systems, or models, like ChatGPT on, remain a fierce academic battleground. The law often lags behind the behavior of industry.

If you've used AI to answer emails or summarise work for you, you might see ChatGPT as an end justifying the means. However, it perhaps should worry us if the only way to achieve that is by exempting specific corporate entities from laws that apply to everyone else.

Not only could that change the nature of debate around copyright lawsuits like this one, but it has the potential to change the way societies structure their legal system.

Fundamental Questions

Cases like this can throw up thorny questions about the future of legal systems, but they can also question the future of AI models themselves. The *New York Times* believes that ChatGPT threatens the long-term existence of the newspaper. On this point, OpenAI says in its statement that it is collaborating with news organizations to provide novel opportunities in journalism. It says the company's goals are to "support a healthy news ecosystem" and to "be a good partner."

Even if we believe that AI systems are a necessary part of the future for our society, it seems like a bad idea to destroy the sources of data that they were originally trained on. This is a concern shared by creative endeavours like the *New York Times*, authors like George R.R. Martin, and also the online encyclopedia Wikipedia.

Advocates of large-scale data collection—like that used to power large language models (LLMs), the technology underlying AI chatbots such as ChatGPT—argue that AI systems "transform" the data they train on by "learning" from their datasets and then creating something new.

ChatGPT, AI, and the Future of Writing

Effectively, what they mean is that researchers provide data written by people and ask these systems to guess the next words in the sentence, as they would when dealing with a real question from a user. By hiding and then revealing these answers, researchers can provide a binary "yes" or "no" answer that helps push AI systems towards accurate predictions. It's for this reason that LLMs need vast reams of written texts.

If we were to copy the articles from the *New York Times'* website and charge people for access, most people would agree this would be "systematic theft on a mass scale" (as the newspaper's lawsuit puts it). But improving the accuracy of an AI by using data to guide it, as shown above, is more complicated than this.

Firms like OpenAI do not store their training data and so argue that the articles from the *New York Times* fed into the dataset are not actually being reused. A counter-argument to this defense of AI, though, is that there is evidence that systems such as ChatGPT can "leak" verbatim excerpts from their training data. OpenAI says this is a "rare bug."

However, it suggests that these systems do store and memorize some of the data they are trained on—unintentionally—and can regurgitate it verbatim when prompted in specific ways. This would bypass any paywalls a for-profit publication may put in place to protect its intellectual property.

Language Use

But what is likely to have a longer term impact on the way we approach legislation in cases such as these is our use of language. Most AI researchers will tell you that the word "learning" is a very weighty and inaccurate word to use to describe what AI is actually doing.

The question must be asked whether the law in its current form is sufficient to protect and support people as society experiences a massive shift into the AI age. Whether something builds on an existing copyrighted piece of work in a manner different from

| 114

Will ChatGPT Help or Harm Journalists and Journalism?

the original is referred to as "transformative use" and is a defense used by OpenAI.

However, these laws were designed to encourage people to remix, recombine and experiment with work already released into the outside world. The same laws were not really designed to protect multi-billion-dollar technology products that work at a speed and scale many orders of magnitude greater than any human writer could aspire to.

The problems with many of the defenses of large-scale data collection and usage is that they rely on strange uses of the English language. We say that AI "learns," that it "understands," that it can "think." However, these are analogies, not precise technical language.

Just like in 1954, when people looked at the modern equivalent of a broken calculator and called it a "brain," we're using old language to grapple with completely new concepts. No matter what we call it, systems like ChatGPT do not work like our brains, and AI systems don't play the same role in society that people play.

Just as we had to develop new words and a new common understanding of technology to make sense of computers in the 1950s, we may need to develop new language and new laws to help protect our society in the 2020s.

VIEWPOINT

> "*Expertise involves a command of the sources that are recognized as comprising legitimate knowledge in our fields.*"

Information from AI Does Not Meet the Standard of Trustworthiness for Journalism

Blayne Haggart

In this viewpoint, Blayne Haggart argues that although ChatGPT and similar programs may be able to produce writing that resembles work by human journalists, there is one key difference between the two: we know the steps in the journalistic process that make it trustworthy, whereas we do not know where ChatGPT gets its information. The ability to cite sources and evidence is a key part of what makes a news source trustworthy. ChatGPT reaches its conclusions by sorting through data and determining what is most statistically likely without regard for how dependable its sources are. This means it cannot be held to the same standard as empirical human output, such as journalism and academic writing. Blayne Haggart is an associate professor of political science at Brock University in Ontario, Canada.

"Unlike with Academics and Reporters, You Can't Check When ChatGPT's Telling the Truth," by Blayne Haggart, The Conversation, January 30, 2023, https://theconversation.com/unlike-with-academics-and-reporters-you-cant-check-when-chatgpts-telling-the-truth-198463. Licensed under CC BY-ND 4.0 International.

As you read, consider the following questions:

1. How does Haggart say science applies to journalism and academic research?
2. What does Haggart mean by "statistical truth"? What's wrong with this?
3. Why does Haggart believe that those who use ChatGPT in journalism and academic research undermine scientific knowledge?

Of all the reactions elicited by ChatGPT, the chatbot from the American for-profit company OpenAI that produces grammatically correct responses to natural-language queries, few have matched those of educators and academics.

Academic publishers have moved to ban ChatGPT from being listed as a co-author and issue strict guidelines outlining the conditions under which it may be used. Leading universities and schools around the world, from France's renowned Sciences Po to many Australian universities, have banned its use.

These bans are not merely the actions of academics who are worried they won't be able to catch cheaters. This is not just about catching students who copied a source without attribution. Rather, the severity of these actions reflects a question, one that is not getting enough attention in the endless coverage of OpenAI's ChatGPT chatbot: why should we trust anything that it outputs?

This is a vitally important question, as ChatGPT and programs like it can easily be used, with or without acknowledgement, in the information sources that comprise the foundation of our society, especially academia and the news media.

Based on my work on the political economy of knowledge governance, academic bans on ChatGPT's use are a proportionate reaction to the threat ChatGPT poses to our entire information ecosystem. Journalists and academics should be wary of using ChatGPT.

ChatGPT, AI, and the Future of Writing

Based on its output, ChatGPT might seem like just another information source or tool. However, in reality, ChatGPT—or, rather the means by which ChatGPT produces its output—is a dagger aimed directly at their very credibility as authoritative sources of knowledge. It should not be taken lightly.

Trust and Information

Think about why we see some information sources or types of knowledge as more trusted than others. Since the European Enlightenment, we've tended to equate scientific knowledge with knowledge in general.

Science is more than laboratory research: it's a way of thinking that prioritizes empirically based evidence and the pursuit of transparent methods regarding evidence collection and evaluation. And it tends to be the gold standard by which all knowledge is judged.

For example, journalists have credibility because they investigate information, cite sources and provide evidence. Even though sometimes the reporting may contain errors or omissions, that doesn't change the profession's authority.

The same goes for opinion editorial writers, especially academics and other experts because they—we—draw our authority from our status as experts in a subject. Expertise involves a command of the sources that are recognized as comprising legitimate knowledge in our fields.

Most op-eds aren't citation-heavy, but responsible academics will be able to point you to the thinkers and the work they're drawing on. And those sources themselves are built on verifiable sources that a reader should be able to verify for themselves.

Truth and Outputs

Because human writers and ChatGPT seem to be producing the same output—sentences and paragraphs—it's understandable that some people may mistakenly confer this scientifically sourced authority onto ChatGPT's output.

Will ChatGPT Help or Harm Journalists and Journalism?

That both ChatGPT and reporters produce sentences is where the similarity ends. What's most important—the source of authority—is not *what* they produce, but *how* they produce it.

ChatGPT doesn't produce sentences in the same way a reporter does. ChatGPT, and other machine-learning, large language models, may seem sophisticated, but they're basically just complex autocomplete machines. Only instead of suggesting the next word in an email, they produce the most statistically likely words in much longer packages.

These programs repackage others' work as if it were something new. It does not "understand" what it produces.

The justification for these outputs can never be truth. Its truth is the truth of the correlation, that the word "sentence" should always complete the phrase "We finish each other's ..." because it is the most common occurrence, not because it is expressing anything that has been observed.

Because ChatGPT's truth is only a statistical truth, output produced by this program cannot ever be trusted in the same way that we can trust a reporter or an academic's output. It cannot be verified because it has been constructed to create output in a different way than what we usually think of as being "scientific."

You can't check ChatGPT's sources because the source is the statistical fact that most of the time, a set of words tend to follow each other.

No matter how coherent ChatGPT's output may seem, simply publishing what it produces is still the equivalent of letting autocomplete run wild. It's an irresponsible practice because it pretends that these statistical tricks are equivalent to well-sourced and verified knowledge.

Similarly, academics and others who incorporate ChatGPT into their workflow run the existential risk of kicking the entire edifice of scientific knowledge out from underneath themselves.

Because ChatGPT's output is correlation-based, how does the writer know that it is accurate? Did they verify it against actual sources, or does the output simply conform to their personal

ChatGPT, AI, and the Future of Writing

prejudices? And if they're experts in their field, why are they using ChatGPT in the first place?

Knowledge Production and Verification

The point is that ChatGPT's processes give us no way to verify its truthfulness. In contrast, that reporters and academics have a scientific, evidence-based method of producing knowledge serves to validate their work, even if the results might go against our preconceived notions.

The problem is especially acute for academics, given our central role in creating knowledge. Relying on ChatGPT to write even part of a column means they're no longer relying on the scientific authority embedded in verified sources.

Instead, by resorting to statistically generated text, they are effectively making an argument from authority. Such actions also mislead the reader, because the reader can't distinguish between text by an author and an AI.

ChatGPT may produce seemingly legible knowledge, as if by magic. But we would be well advised not to mistake its output for actual, scientific knowledge. One should never confuse coherence with understanding.

ChatGPT promises easy access to new and existing knowledge, but it is a poisoned chalice. Readers, academics and reporters beware.

| 120

Periodical and Internet Sources Bibliography

The following articles have been selected to supplement the diverse views presented in this chapter.

Karen Blum, "Tip Sheet: Harnessing ChatGPT for Good Journalistic Use," Association of Health Care Journalists, August 31, 2023. https://healthjournalism.org/blog/2023/08/tip-sheet-harnessing-chatgpt-for-good-journalistic-use/.

Caitlin Dewey, "11 Practical and Responsible Ways I have Improved My Journalism with AI," Poynter Institute, October 3, 2023. https://www.poynter.org/tech-tools/2023/how-to-use-chatgpt-journalism/.

Khaled Diab, "What Future for Journalism in the Age of AI?" Al Jazeera, July 19, 2023. https://www.aljazeera.com/opinions/2023/7/19/what-future-for-journalism-in-the-age-of-ai.

Jade Drummond, "Newsrooms Around the World Are Using AI to Optimize Work, Despite Concerns About Bias and Accuracy," the Verge, September 28, 2023. https://www.theverge.com/2023/9/28/23894651/ai-newsroom-journalism-study-automation-bias.

Samantha Floreani, "Is Artificial Intelligence a Threat to Journalism or Will the Technology Destroy Itself?" the *Guardian*, August 5, 2023. https://www.theguardian.com/commentisfree/2023/aug/05/is-mutant-news-headed-our-way-or-will-ai-chatbots-eat-their-own-tails.

Robin Guess, "How AI Could Act as Boost for Investigative Journalism," Voice of America, January 10, 2024. https://www.voanews.com/a/how-ai-could-act-as-boost-for-investigative-journalism/7434364.html.

Will Henshall, "Experts Warn Congress of Dangers AI Poses to Journalism," *Time*, January 10, 2024. https://time.com/6554118/congress-ai-journalism-hearing/.

John Herrman, "How Will Artificial Intelligence Change the News Business?" *New York Magazine*, August 1, 2023. https://nymag.com/intelligencer/2023/08/how-ai-will-change-the-news-business.html.

ChatGPT, AI, and the Future of Writing

Mathew Ingram, "ChatGPT, Artificial Intelligence, and the News," *Columbia Journalism Review,* April 13, 2023. https://www.cjr.org/the_media_today/chatgpt_ai_fears_media.php.

Jeff Israely, "How Will Journalists Use ChatGPT? Clues from a Newsroom That's Been Using AI for Years," Nieman Lab, March 1, 2023. https://www.niemanlab.org/2023/03/how-will-journalists-use-chatgpt-clues-from-a-newsroom-thats-been-using-ai-for-years/.

Farhad Manjoo, "ChatGPT Is Already Changing How I Do My Job," the *New York Times*, April 21, 2023. https://www.nytimes.com/2023/04/21/opinion/chatgpt-journalism.html.

Gabby Miller, "Senate Hearing on AI and the Future of Journalism," Tech Policy Press, January 11, 2024. https://www.techpolicy.press/senate-hearing-on-ai-and-the-future-of-journalism/.

Chapter 4

Will ChatGPT Help or Harm Creative Writers?

Chapter Preface

In this chapter we turn our attention from journalists and students to a different kind of writer: the creative writer. Creative writing is generally defined as writing that goes beyond the facts and brings a certain insight or stance of the author to the work. Creative writing is usually, but not always, fiction. Academic writing is not creative writing, nor is, in most cases, journalism. But memoir can be creative writing as well as some other types of non-fiction—for example, a meditation on the emotional impact of climate change.

ChatGPT's effect on creative writers is different from its effect on those whose work is more fact-oriented, and the authors here dig into those differences. Since ChatGPT isn't going anywhere anytime soon, some of the authors here think the best approach is to learn to make the best of it. Writers might even harness AI to help them become better writers.

The first viewpoint focuses primarily on copywriters—writers who write advertisements or scripts for television commercials, websites, emails, and so on. These writers are mostly optimistic. They think that writers, if they are to survive, must team up with ChatGPT rather than resist it. The next author, who addresses the role ChatGPT can play in the editorial process for fictional works, suggests that it could be a useful tool for human editors as well.

In the third viewpoint, the author looks at issues of quality and intellectual property in AI-generated fictional works. The next viewpoint follows up with a gloomy perspective: AI won't replace the creative author, but will replace the work those authors do to make money. (Few authors make a living writing fiction.)

The final viewpoint, however, offers some hope. It's about how authors are fighting back—and why they might just win.

VIEWPOINT 1

> *"It's early days for these scary and exciting tools and they will affect every creative person's job. "*

Creative Writers Must Learn to Work with ChatGPT

Olivia Atkins

In this viewpoint, Olivia Atkins rounds up opinions from several people who work as creative writers to get their perspectives of how ChatGPT might—or might not—harm creative writers. These writers work as copywriters, meaning they write the text for advertisements or other types of marketing. In general, those surveyed believe that ChatGPT can be a useful tool in the copywriting process, and that the future holds a peaceful partnership between AI and human copywriters. Olivia Atkins is a freelance writer and journalist based in London.

As you read, consider the following questions:

1. Why does James Devon think copywriters' jobs are safe?
2. What lesson does Tim Riley take from the story of Civil War General John Sedgwick?
3. Why is Micky Tudor excited about this technology?

"ChatGPT: A Creative Tool Or A Threat To Human Creativity?" by Olivia Atkins, Creative Salon. Reprinted with permission.

ChatGPT, AI, and the Future of Writing

Ryan Reynolds' experiment with AI-assisted chatbot ChatGPT made headlines earlier this month after he tested its ability to write an ad script for his mobile virtual network provider, Mobile Mint. And it wasn't terrible.

But even Reynolds admitted that its work was both "mildly-terrifying and compelling."

So what does this spell for the industry and creativity at large; should writers in particular (and creatives in general) worry that they'll be out of a job in future? Or can the tech be useful at ideation stage? And more importantly, how can we better prioritize and value human creativity to utilize new tech as a complementary tool rather than see it as a threat to human capabilities?

Will Lion, Joint Chief Strategy Officer at BBH London

First a threat, then a tool but after that just table stakes. If computers are bicycles for the mind, ChatGPT is a motorbike letting us go creatively further, faster with less effort. The rub comes when everyone has motorbikes. Neural networks trained on the same dataset will give the same outputs. That's just how they work. To find creative edge you'd have to either have more compute power to get there first, train it on a hand-tuned dataset or get really good at asking AI questions (cue Prompt Strategists in the 2020s). Just as an agency with Google beats one without it, so an agency with ChatGPT beats one without it. But when everyone has it, human ingenuity must re-engage again to find the uncharted space. As the Red Queen tells Alice (in Wonderland) when everyone is running "It takes all the running you can do, to keep in the same place. If you want to get somewhere else, you must run at least twice as fast as that!" In the end, creativity levels up.

Jonothan Hunt, Senior Creative Technologist, Wunderman Thompson

I'm getting this question a lot at the moment with the emergence of more mainstream AI tools that don't just generate content but can refine it through intuitive interfaces or even dialogue, at speed.

Will ChatGPT Help or Harm Creative Writers?

This is not new; ML/AI-powered tools in our creative software suites have made tasks like rotoscoping, feature selection, style transfer, feature-based cropping, resizing for different formats and so much more, happen instantaneously where before they might've taken hours, even weeks, or not even been practical. Now creatives use these tools every day.

Tools like ChatGPT are having such an impact because they don't just assist in creation—they help with research, ideation and even prototyping too. Pretty much all the tangible "outputs" of a creative. Just look at integrations of ChatGPT in places like You.com—for me and many others, a good proportion of traditional internet searches have been replaced by these tools and their ability to understand complex questions, generate readable insights from a bunch of information and even create new content (including code!).

It's my opinion that creatives should know what these tools do and how to work with them, as well as understanding at least a little about how they work. And that's not because creatives will be replaced; whilst these tools can be great at creating all of the above at scale, people remain better at topical cultural nuance both in the contexts of the audiences they're creating for, and as importantly the people they're selling their ideas to.

I think we remain in a space where the work that these tools can better us at is work that we should have the option to be freed from, so we can focus on what we're really good at. Instead of spending ages trying to find the right search to get the perfect insight, why not come up with some thought starters with ChatGPT? Instead of scrolling through countless stock images that you'll end up tweaking anyway for a scamp, why not brief an AI model for exactly what you want and use your time to refine the idea or different executions of it? Instead of writing believable text or using Lorem Ipsum for a site you're designing, why not use any one of the many AI writing tools out there?

Looking into the next few years, we'll see these models continue to automate heavily templated stuff like product-focused retargeting campaigns where countless combinations of content can be generated and tested to achieve more and better-quality clicks. More interesting to me however, will be watching as the creative industry is able to focus on making and selling more daring ideas.

There's so much more for creatives specifically to be thinking about, from ethics (what is the training data for these models? Is my work being used? What's the difference between me being vs. an AI model being inspired by someone else's work? Who should decide what's ethical? Users? Platforms? Governments?), to competition with other creatives (am I as effective as others who've learnt to work with and prompt these tools? Demand for more ideas and executions in a bunch of different formats ain't going away!)

James Devon, Chief Strategy Officer, MBAstack

It's hard to have a play with ChatGPT and not think it's remarkable. I absolutely don't think it's the sole answer and I think we can assure copywriters their jobs are safe. However, I have seen ways how it can be helpful in our work.

1. Thought-starter generation. AI may not be brilliant output straight off the bat, but wonderful for generation without judgment. I can see ChatGPT being used in many a proposition generation session, in name generation or even as a starting point for headlines.

2. Summarizing articles. Our client work at MBAstack takes us from flowers to mail to pet care to accounting to cheese. That's a lot to be an expert on—previously I was only ever an expert on cheese. Taking essays and other functional outputs, I've found ChatGPT to be a worthy summarizer.

3. Editing to a word count. Another classic task. Disaster, I've done the classic planner tactic of writing 116 words, when we needed it under 100. ChatGPT proves much easier than the editing of my own verbose phraseology.

| 128

4. Changing the tone of voice. We need our paragraph to be more inspiring. Let's add some rousing tone of voice. Can an AI add a bit of hope? A bit of Obama "yes we can"? Yes, it can.

Clearly, such an important part of our line of work is the generation and iteration of thoughts and phrases. Whether the AI comes up with the right answer is not the point—it can help provide the stimulus for us to build on or select the most interesting direction. I'm on the side of it being a complementary tool, rather than a threat.

Katy Wright, Chief Executive Officer, FCB Inferno

We all said we're terrified but equally WOW (wish I'd had this for my homework!)

For me it just shows what's possible and frankly how it's not subscription based I've no clue (no doubt it will be). I think about how much that just enriches what we offer clients and how the boundaries of tech should support and frankly I'm excited and terrified but I love that feeling.

I don't think writers should worry (just try asking it a joke!) they should see it complementing nay pushing, providing a starting off point.

Also quality comes down to questions you ask and thinking behind them . . . also current data (as a lot of these platforms are not live thinking openai is based on 2021 data points).

Technology is and has always been to make things easier/ better, so embracing change has always been the way forward or we'd still be on the savannah rather than considering space travel!

Tim Riley, Creative Partner, AMV BBDO

On May 9 1864, the Union General John Sedgwick and his infantrymen came under fire from Confederate snipers at Spotsylvania in Virginia. As the men took cover, Sedgwick strode back and forth, declaring: "They couldn't hit an elephant at this distance." Moments later, he was mortally wounded when a bullet

ChatGPT, AI, and the Future of Writing

struck him below the left eye. Any creative pronouncing that AI doesn't pose a threat to their livelihood is risking a similar act of hubris.

Yet, while AI has come on in leaps and bounds recently, it's still a work in progress. As Ian Leslie pointed out recently in his excellent Substack, "The Ruffian," work created by bots tends towards "the generic, bland and superficial. What we have here, for now at least, is a machine for generating plausible bullshit." He goes on to point out that this isn't necessarily a bad thing. "Anyone's first draft is essentially a piece of bullshit. ChatGPT may prove a useful tool in the early stage of a creative project, enabling us to get more quickly to better ideas."

My instinct is that AI creatives will probably co-exist with the human variety. New technologies don't automatically replace everything that's come before them. YouTube hasn't replaced television. Television, in turn, didn't replace radio. Though of course, I would say that, wouldn't I? Ask a chatbot and you may get a different answer. For the moment, ChatGPT and its ilk still can't hit the elephant. But they're getting closer.

Alan Young, Chief Creative Officer, St Luke's

We need to see AI as a builder would see the steam-shovel at the time of the Industrial revolution. In the way those machines augmented human muscle, AI will augment the human mind—boosting productivity, and saving time.

With Ryan Reynolds' Mint Mobile ad, the idea is its means of production. It isn't what we'd call a concept and ChatGPT can be used conceptually.

On a pitch a fortnight ago and I gave it two briefs.

One, to re-name the technology inside the product. It made a series of suggestions every bit as good as the ones our project team members made.

Two, to generate a series of funny scenarios based on the product's USP. Its first efforts weren't exactly rib-tickling, but refining of the instructions resulted in one scenario that formed the basis of one of five scripts we pitched.

It's worth remembering the quality of ChatGPT's answers depends on the clarity of your instructions. It doesn't have imagination, it just helps bring your imagination to life. Neither does it know when the answer is good—you decide that.

It's early days for these scary and exciting tools and they will affect every creative person's job. We've only got one option—work out how they can make us smarter and stay smarter.

Micky Tudor, Chief Creative Officer, The&Partnership

One evening, five years ago, was one of my most nerve-wracking moments in advertising.

I was waiting for a client script to arrive in my inbox. After months of preparation, an AI learning tool was about to spit out its script. One script. One "right" answer was that we were going to shoot exactly as written, whatever it was. I needn't have worried. The script would turn out to be eerily coherent—a car escaping its own imminent test crash. The project piqued the interest of Oscar-winning director Kevin McDonald and clients were invited to talk about the project on news outlets.

Five years later what has changed? There is still the sense of denial from some, and of wonder and experimentation from others, but this is beginning to give way to an impending sense of practicality. This year we will incorporate AI into workflows and the creative process more formally. Whether that be for thought starters, for inspiration, to get to ideas faster, or help look at an idea from a different angle.

And that's exciting. Creativity finds inspiration and serendipity in all sorts of weird, wonderful and unexpected places. Technology is just one of them.

ChatGPT, AI, and the Future of Writing

Drew Spencer, Executive Experience Design Director, adam&eveDDB

We've been worried about robots taking our jobs for decades. This is not new. And as robust and compelling as ChatGPT is, it's not a true threat to human creativity. We shouldn't think of it as a substitute. We should be excited about it! It's the first really useful tool that AI has produced and we should embrace it for the opportunity it represents. They say there's no such thing as an original idea—ChatGPT embodies this concept. It's an emulator, built on everything that's already been written down somewhere. It's the ultimate magpie. It emulates us. It finds the patterns in our past and weaves them together in ways that feel magical but aren't original. I believe that it can add value to the creative process, but it will never compete with the limitless realm of human expression. It writes the kind of ideas that ECDs knock back because they're just "missing something." So let's use it that way. To kick off a brainstorm. To get to "the idea before the idea." Fast research for manifestos, straplines, headlines & scripts. It's a great way to simplify and/or speed up certain processes that have needed reinventing for years. But ChatGPT won't replace creatives. It doesn't get goosebumps. It has no hair on the back of its neck to stand up when the energy changes in the room. It's never felt that rush of adrenaline when it smashes one out of the park.

Tim Clegg, Executive Creative Director, Digitas UK

We in the creative community have long thought AI could never replace human ingenuity and craft. But systems like ChatGPT and Dall•E have knocked our collective apathy for six. And rightly so. They will undoubtedly shake things up.

It was when our creative tech guru showed me a children's book he'd had written and illustrated in under a minute that the penny dropped for me. Sam isn't a writer or an illustrator, but in his coffee break he had become both. Sure, it wasn't Julia Donaldson and Axel Scheffler. But that misses the point. The process may be different but it's still one that rewards creativity. In the hands of someone with fresh ideas and an appreciation of craft, AI can be a game-changer.

If you're in the business of knocking out functional copy for undemanding clients, then this could be a threat. But creatives like Sam, who'll help define creativity over the next decade, are already asking themselves the more important question: "how can I use this to be more creative?" And what could be more human than that?

VIEWPOINT 2

> *"ChatGPT can give credible-sounding editorial feedback. But we recommend editors and authors don't ask it to give individual assessments or expert interventions any time soon."*

ChatGPT Does Not Understand Fiction the Way Good Editors Do

Katherine Day, Renée Otmar, Rose Michael, and Sharon Mullins

In this viewpoint, the authors walk through the process of having ChatGPT edit a fictional story and compare it to the work of human editors to see if it is able to improve the quality of the story in a way that resembles current editorial practices. The authors found that ChatGPT tends to offer correct but unoriginal and vague advice, and when it is asked to offer more specific feedback it suggests replacing original writing with work that is more cliched. However, ChatGPT can be a useful in identifying issues with verb tense, punctuation, and grammar. While the authors argue that ChatGPT cannot match the experience, cultural knowledge, and emotional intelligence that makes human editors successful, they do believe it can be used as a tool. Katherine Day is a lecturer in publishing at the University of Melbourne in Australia, where Sharon Mullins is a tutor in publishing

"Can ChatGPT edit fiction? 4 professional editors asked AI to do their job – and it ruined their short story," by Katherine Day, Renée Otmar, Rose Michael, and Sharon Mullins, The Conversation, February 12, 2024, https://theconversation.com/can-chatgpt-edit-fiction-4-professional-editors-asked-ai-to-do-their-job-and-it-ruined-their-short-story-216631. Licensed under CC BY-ND 4.0 International.

| 134

and editing. Renée Otmar is an honorary research fellow in the faculty of health at Deakin University, and Rose Michael is a senior lecturer and BA program manager in creative writing at RMIT University, both of which are also in Australia.

As you read, consider the following questions:

1. Was ChatGPT able to tell that the story had already been published? What concern does this raise?
2. Why did the authors find ChatGPT's advice in the second (rewrite) phase unhelpful?
3. How do the authors explain ChattGPT's writing preferences?

Writers have been using AI tools for years—from Microsoft Word's spellcheck (which often makes unwanted corrections) to the passive-aggressive Grammarly. But ChatGPT is different.

ChatGPT's natural language processing enables a dialogue, much like a conversation—albeit with a slightly odd acquaintance. And it can generate vast amounts of copy, quickly, in response to queries posed in ordinary, everyday language. This suggests, at least superficially, it can do some of the work a book editor does.

We are professional editors, with extensive experience in the Australian book publishing industry, who wanted to know how ChatGPT would perform when compared to a human editor. To find out, we decided to ask it to edit a short story that had already been worked on by human editors—and we compared the results.

The Experiment: ChatGPT vs. Human Editors

The story we chose, "The Ninch" (written by Rose), had gone through three separate rounds of editing, with four human editors (and a typesetter).

ChatGPT, AI, and the Future of Writing

The first version had been rejected by literary journal *Overland,* but its fiction editor, Claire Corbett, had given generous feedback. The next version received detailed advice from freelance editor Nicola Redhouse, a judge of the *Big Issue* fiction edition (which had shortlisted the story). Finally, the piece found a home at another literary journal, *Meanjin,* where deputy editor Tess Smurthwaite incorporated comments from the issue's freelance editor and also their typesetter in her correspondence.

We had a wealth of human feedback to compare ChatGPT's recommendations with.

We used a standard, free ChatGPT generative AI tool for our edits, which we conducted as separate series of prompts designed to assess the scope and success of AI as an editorial tool.

We wanted to see if ChatGPT could develop and fine tune this unpublished work—and if so, whether it would do it in a way that resembled current editorial practice. By comparing it with human examples, we tried to determine where and at what stage in the process ChatGPT might be most successful as an editorial tool.

The story includes expressive descriptions, poetic imagery, strong symbolism and a subtle subtext. It explores themes of motherhood, nature, and hints at deeper mysteries.

We chose it because we believe the literary genre, with its play and experimentation, poetry and lyricism, offers rich pickings for complex editorial conversations. (And because we knew we could get permission from all participants in the process to share their feedback.)

In the story, a mother reflects on her untamed, sea-loving child. Supernatural possibilities are hinted at before the tale turns closer to home, ending with the mother revealing her own divergent nature—and looping back to offer more meaning to the title:

> *pinching the skin between my toes ... Making each digit its own unique peninsula.*

Round 1: The First Draft

We started with a simple, general prompt, assuming the least amount of editorial guidance from the author. (Authors submitting stories to magazines and journals generally don't give human editors a detailed, prescriptive brief.)

Our initial prompt for all three examples was: "Hi ChatGPT, could I please ask for your editorial suggestions on my short story, which I'd like to submit for publication in a literary journal?"

Responding to the first version of the story, ChatGPT provided a summary of key themes (motherhood, connection to nature, the mysteries of the ocean) and made a list of editorial suggestions.

Interestingly, ChatGPT did not pick up that the story was now published and attributed to an author. Raising questions about its ability, or inclination, to identify plagiarism. Nor did it define the genre, which is one of the first assessments an editor makes.

ChatGPT's suggestions were: to add more description of the coastal setting, provide more physical description of the characters, break up long paragraphs to make the piece more reader-friendly, add more dialogue for characterization and insight, make the sentences shorter, reveal more inner thoughts of the characters, expand on the symbolism, show don't tell, incorporate foreshadowing earlier, and provide resolution rather than ending on a mystery.

All good, if stock standard, advice.

ChatGPT also suggested reconsidering the title—clearly not making the connection between mother and daughter's ocean affinity and their webbed toes—and reading the story aloud to help identify awkward phrasing, pacing and structure.

While this wasn't particularly helpful feedback, it was not technically wrong.

ChatGPT picked up on the major themes and main characters. And the advice for more foreshadowing, dialogue and description, along with shorter paragraphs and an alternative ending, was generally sound.

ChatGPT, AI, and the Future of Writing

In fact, it echoed the usual feedback you'd get from a creative writing workshop, or the kind of advice offered in books on the writing craft.

They are the sort of suggestions an editor might write in response to almost any text—not particularly specific to this story, or to our stated aim of submitting it to a literary publication.

Stage Two: AI (Re)Writes

Next, we provided a second prompt, responding to ChatGPT's initial feedback—attempting to emulate the back-and-forth discussions that are a key part of the editorial process.

We asked ChatGPT to take a more practical, interventionist approach and rework the text in line with its own editorial suggestions:

Thank you for your feedback about uneven pacing. Could you please suggest places in the story where the pace needs to speed up or slow down? Thank you too for the feedback about imagery and description. Could you please suggest places where there is too much imagery and it needs more action storytelling instead?

That's where things fell apart.

ChatGPT offered a radically shorter, changed story. The atmospheric descriptions, evocative imagery and nods towards (unspoken) mystery were replaced with unsubtle phrases—which Rose swears she would never have written, or signed off on.

Lines added included: "my daughter has always been an enigma to me", "little did I know" and "a sense of unease washed over me." Later in the story, this phrasing was clumsily suggested a second time: "relief washed over me."

The author's unique descriptions were changed to familiar cliches: "rugged beauty," "roar of the ocean," "unbreakable bond." ChatGPT also changed the text from Australian English (which all Australian publications require) to U.S. spelling and style ("realization", "mom").

In summary, a story where a mother sees her daughter as a "southern selkie going home" (phrasing that hints at a speculative subtext) on a rocky outcrop and really sees her (in all possible,

| 138

playful senses of that word) was changed to a fishing tale, where a (definitely human) girl arrives home holding up, we kid you not, "a shiny fish."

It became hard to give credence to any of ChatGPT's advice.

Esteemed editor Bruce Sims once advised it's not an editor's job to fix things; it's an editor's job to point out what needs fixing. But if you are asked to be a hands-on editor, your revisions must be an improvement on the original—not just different. And certainly not worse.

It is our industry's maxim, too, to first do no harm. Not only did ChatGPT not improve Rose's story, it made it worse.

What Did the Human Editors Do?

ChatGPT's edit did not come close to the calibre of insight and editorial know-how offered by Overland editor Claire Corbett. Some examples:

> *There's some beautiful writing and fantastic themes, but the quotes about drowning are heavy-handed; they're given the job of foreshadowing suspense, creating unease in the reader, rather than the narrator doing that job.*
>
> *The biggest problem is that final transition—I don't know how to read the narrator. Her emotions don't seem to fit the situation.*
>
> *For me stories are driven by choices and I'm not clear what decision our narrator, or anyone else, in the story faces.*
>
> *It's entirely possible I'm not getting something important, but I think that if I'm not getting it, our readers won't either.*

Freelance editor Nicola, who has a personal relationship with Rose, went even further in her exchange (in response to the next draft, where Rose had attempted to address the issues Claire identified). She pushed Rose to work and rework the last sentence until they both felt the language lock in and land.

> *I'm not 100% sold on this line. I think it's a little confusing . . . It might just be too much hinted at in too subtle a way for the reader.*

ChatGPT, AI, and the Future of Writing

Originally, the final sentence read: "Ready to make my slower way back to the house, retracing—overwriting—any sign of my own less-than more-than normal prints."

The final version is: "Ready to make my slower way back to the house, retracing, overwriting, any sign of my own less-than, more-than, normal prints." With the addition of a final standalone line: "I have seen what I wanted to see: her, me, free."

Claire and Nicola's feedback show how an editor is a story's ideal reader. A good editor can guide the author through problems with point of view and emotional dynamics—going beyond the simple mechanics of grammar, sentence length and the number of adjectives.

In other words, they demonstrate something we call editorial intelligence.

ChatGPT Reflects Our Biases

Systems like ChatGPT have produced outputs that are nonsensical, factually incorrect—even sexist, racist, or otherwise offensive. These negative outputs have not shocked Timnit Gebru, the founder and executive director of the Distributed Artificial Intelligence Research Institute.

Gebru's research has pointed to the pitfalls of training artificial intelligence applications with mountains of indiscriminate data from the internet. In 2020, she co-authored a paper highlighting the risks of certain AI systems. This publication, she said, led her to being forced out as the co-head of Google's AI ethics team.

As Gebru explained, people can assume that, because the internet is replete with text and data, systems trained on this data must therefore be encoding various viewpoints.

"And what we argue is that size doesn't guarantee diversity," Gebru said.

Instead, she contends, there are many ways data on the internet can enforce bias—beginning with who has access to the internet and who does not. Furthermore, women and people in underrepresented

Editorial intelligence is akin to emotional intelligence. It incorporates intellectual, creative and emotional capital—all gained from lived experience, complemented by technical skills and industry expertise, applied through the prism of human understanding.

Skills include confident conviction, based on deep accumulated knowledge, meticulous research, cultural mediation and social skills. (After all, the author doesn't have to do what we say—ours is a persuasive profession.)

Round 2: The Revised Story

Next, we submitted a revised draft that had addressed Claire's suggestions and incorporated the conversations with Nicola.

groups are more likely to be harassed and bullied online, leading them to spend less time on the internet, Gebru said. In turn, these perspectives are less represented in the data that large language models encode.

[…]

To combat this, Gebru said companies and research groups are building toxicity detectors that are similar to social media platforms that do content moderation. That task ultimately falls to humans who train the system on which content is harmful.

To Gebru, this piecemeal approach—removing harmful content as it happens—is like playing whack-a-mole. She thinks the way to handle artificial intelligence systems like these going forward is to build in oversight and regulation.

"I do think that there should be an agency that is helping us make sure that some of these systems are safe, that they're not harming us, that it is actually beneficial, you know?" Gebru said. "There should be some sort of oversight. I don't see any reason why this one industry is being treated so differently from everything else."

[…]

"ChatGPT and large language model bias" by CBS Broadcasting Inc., March 5, 2023

ChatGPT, AI, and the Future of Writing

This draft was submitted with the same initial prompt: "Hi ChatGPT, could I please ask for your editorial suggestions on my short story, which I'd like to submit for publication in a literary journal?"

ChatGPT responded with a summary of themes and editorial suggestions very similar to what it had offered in the first round. Again, it didn't pick up that the story had already been published, nor did it clearly identify the genre.

For the follow-up, we asked specifically for an edit that corrected any issues with tense, spelling and punctuation.

It was a laborious process: the 2,500-word piece had to be submitted in chunks of 300–500 words and the revised sections manually combined.

However, these simpler editorial tasks were clearly more in ChatGPT's ballpark. When we created a document (in Microsoft Word) that compared the original and AI-edited versions, the flagged changes appeared very much like a human editor's tracked changes.

But ChatGPT's changes revealed its own writing preferences, which didn't allow for artistic play and experimentation. For example, it reinstated prepositions like "in", "at", "of" and "to", which slowed down the reading and reduced the creativity of the piece—and altered the writing style.

This makes sense when you know the datasets that drive ChatGPT mean it explicitly works toward the word most likely to come next. (This might be directed differently in the future, towards more creative, and less stable or predictable models.)

Round 3: Our Final Submission

In the third and final round of the experiment, we submitted the draft that had been accepted by *Meanjin*.

The process kicked off with the same initial prompt: "Hi ChatGPT, could I please ask for your editorial suggestions on my short story, which I'd like to submit for publication in a literary journal?"

| 142

Again, ChatGPT offered its rote list of editorial suggestions. (Was this even editing?)

This time, we followed up with separate prompts for each element we wanted ChatGPT to review: title, pacing, imagery/description.

ChatGPT came back with suggestions for how to revise specific parts of the text, but the suggestions were once again formulaic. There was no attempt to offer—or support—any decision to go against familiar tropes.

Many of ChatGPT's suggestions—much like the machine rewrites earlier—were heavy-handed. The alternative titles, like "Seaside Solitude" and "Coastal Connection," used cringeworthy alliteration.

In contrast, *Meanjin*'s editor Tess Smurthwaite—on behalf of herself, copyeditor Richard McGregor, and typesetter Patrick Cannon—offered light revisions:

> *The edits are relatively minimal, but please feel free to reject anything that you're not comfortable with.*
>
> *Our typesetter has queried one thing: on page 100, where "Not like a thing at all" has become a new para. He wants to know whether the quote marks should change. Technically, I'm thinking that we should add a closing one after "not a thing" and then an opening one on the next line, but I'm also worried it might read like the new para is a response, and that it hasn't been said by Elsie. Let me know what you think.*

Sometimes editorial expertise shows itself in not changing a text. Different isn't necessarily good. It takes an expert to recognize when a story is working just fine. If it ain't broke, don't fix it.

It also takes a certain kind of aerial, bird's-eye view to notice when the way type is set creates ambiguities in the text. Typesetters really are akin to editors.

The Verdict: Can ChatGPT Edit?

So, ChatGPT can give credible-sounding editorial feedback. But we recommend editors and authors don't ask it to give individual assessments or expert interventions any time soon.

ChatGPT, AI, and the Future of Writing

A major problem that emerged early in this experiment involved ethics: ChatGPT did not ask for or verify the authorship of our story. A journal or magazine would ask an author to confirm a text is their own original work at some stage in the process: either at submission or contract stage.

A freelance editor would likely use other questions to determine the same answer—and in the process of asking about the author's plans for publication, they would also determine the author's own stylistic preferences.

Human editors demonstrate their credentials through their work history, and keep their experience up-to-date with professional training and qualifications.

What might the ethics be, we wonder, of giving the same recommendations to every author asking for editing advice? You might be disgruntled to receive generic feedback if you expect or have paid for individual engagement.

As we've seen, when writing challenges expected conventions, AI struggles to respond. Its primary function is to appropriate, amalgamate and regurgitate—which is not enough when it comes to editing literary fiction.

Literary writing aims to—and often does—convey so much more than what the words on screen explicitly say. Literary writers strive for evocative, original prose that draws upon subtext and calls up undercurrents, making the most of nuance and implication to create imagined realities and invent unreal worlds.

At this stage of ChatGPT's development, literally following the advice of its editing tools to edit literary fiction is likely to make it worse, not better.

In Rose's case, her oceanic allegory about difference, with a nod to the supernatural, was turned into a story about a fish.

ChatGPT Is 'Like the New Intern'

This experiment shows how AI and human editors could work together. AI suggestions can be scrutinized—and integrated or dismissed—by authors or editors during the creative process.

| 144

And while many of its suggestions were not that useful, AI efficiently identified issues with tense, spelling and punctuation (within an overly narrow interpretation of these rules).

Without human editorial intelligence, ChatGPT does more harm than help. But when used by human editors, it's like any other tool—as good, or bad, as the tradesperson who wields it.

VIEWPOINT 3

> *"If we allow AI to commandeer the arts, whether in literature, music, or film, it could mean the erasure of authentic human expression. And if there is any real purpose to art, it is to sincerely communicate what is most profound about the human condition."*

AI Takes the Soul Out of Creative Writing

C. G. Jones

In this viewpoint, C. G. Jones discusses several of the issues with AI-generated writing. For one, he notes that the quality of the writing tends to be quite low. But beyond that, there's the issue of the creative and intellectual property of creative writers. Jones discusses a case in which Amazon listed five books by the author Jane Friedman that were actually created by AI. Since Friedman did not own the trademark for her name, Amazon refused to remove the AI-generated books. AI can steal real authors' names and work to create "new" books, but Jones believes they will always be lower quality because they lack the mark of human creativity. C. G. Jones is an author, journalist, and weekend editor for the Blaze.

"AI Is Coming for Art's Soul" by C.G. Jones, Intellectual Takeout, September 1, 2023, https://intellectualtakeout.org/2023/09/ai-is-coming-for-arts-soul/. Licensed under CC BY 4.0 International.

As you read, consider the following questions:

1. Why does Jones believe that AI-generated writing could destroy someone's reputation?
2. In what sense does AI-generated work present a new era of fake news and misinformation?
3. What does Jones think is one reason AI writes poorly?

While AI-based technology has recently been used to summon deepfakes and create a disturbing outline for running a death camp, the ever-pervasive digital juggernaut has also been used to write books under the byline of well-known authors.

The *Guardian* recently reported five books appeared for sale on Amazon that were apparently written by author Jane Friedman. Only, they weren't written by Friedman at all: They were written by AI. When Friedman submitted a claim to Amazon, Amazon said they would not remove the books because she had not trademarked her name.

Though the books were eventually taken down, Friedman said the books were "if not wholly generated by AI, then at least mostly generated by AI." She went on to say, "It feels like a violation, because it's really low quality material with my name on it." She explained: "It looks terrible. It makes me look like I'm trying to take advantage of people with really crappy books."

The books' low quality is just one of many issues involving this emerging phenomenon. It suggests anyone who knows how to man AI technology could publish virtually anything under anyone's name, and there would be nothing the author could do about it until the damage was already done. It is easy to imagine how this technology could be used to destroy someone's reputation.

The trouble continues. The creative and intellectual property of creatives is suddenly put in jeopardy by so-called digital progress, and it presents a new era of fake news and overt misinformation. In

ChatGPT, AI, and the Future of Writing

a world where it is already difficult to parse truth from falsehood, this technology could make it near impossible to decipher what is really happening in the world.

There is also the concern over identity theft, which appears to have happened to Friedman. If Amazon and other major platforms refuse to implement a system that can effectively identify an author, then what would prevent someone from using AI to publish material under a well-known name?

"Unless Amazon puts some sort of policy in place to prevent anyone from just uploading whatever book they want and applying whatever name they want, this will continue, it's not going to end with me," Friedman said. "They have no procedure for reporting this sort of activity where someone's trying to profit off someone's name."

This situation also presents a serious issue for those of us who read. Friedman mentioned the books published under her name were poorly written. One reason AI writes poorly written books is because it wholly lacks the unique watermark of human thought and emotion. While we consume art for a multitude of reasons, I believe what we are really after is another individual's idiosyncratic perspective and expression.

If we allow AI to commandeer the arts, whether in literature, music, or film, it could mean the erasure of authentic human expression. And if there is any real purpose to art, it is to sincerely communicate what is most profound about the human condition. These are expressions utterly inaccessible to AI, without recycling pre-existing material created by humans.

AI is profoundly incapable of producing Mozart's "Jupiter Symphony," Christopher Nolan's *Oppenheimer*, or Shakespeare's *Hamlet*. The reason why these works of art are so successful is, in part, because humans—with all their genius, flaws, and idiosyncrasies—made them. A hunk of technology—no matter how intelligent—simply lacks the twinkle of humanity necessary for a meaningful piece of art.

Will ChatGPT Help or Harm Creative Writers?

Though AI probably isn't going anywhere, I still hold out hope that we will recognize its limitations to elevate and connect us through art. In our lonely modern era, what we need is more human connection, not less.

VIEWPOINT 4

> "It is all too apparent that artists,
> writers, and performers cannot avoid
> the threat presented to their work
> by AI."

AI Won't Mean the Death of the Author, Just the Starvation of the Artist

Terry Flew

This viewpoint was written in 2023 during the writers' and actors' strike. There were several reasons for the strike, but AI was one. Here Terry Flew uses the strike as a starting place for discussing how ChatGPT and similar programs will affect creative writers and other artists. Most people working in creative industries, such as creative writers, struggle to make a living from their creative craft, and AI threatens to reduce the opportunities for paid work even more. Terry Flew is a professor of digital communication and culture at the University of Sydney in Australia.

As you read, consider the following questions:

1. How has the threat of AI changed since 2000, according to this viewpoint?
2. Was Flew surprised that AI is posing a threat to creative writers?

"Creative AI: The death of the author?" by Terry Flew, The University of Sydney, August 2023, https://sbi.sydney.edu.au/creative-ai-the-death-of-the-author/. Licensed under CC BY-ND.

| 150

3. Why is the fact that AI cannot do creative work not reassuring to the artists who do?

The long running strike action by the Writers Guild of America against the Alliance of Motion Picture and Television Producers, which was more recently joined by the Screen Actors Guild, has drawn attention to the role of artificial intelligence in the future of film and television productions. Given the speed and significance of developments in generative artificial intelligence, they are right to be concerned, as are all creative workers.

Both the writers and actors are concerned that unless they can secure a binding agreement with the studios, films and TV shows will increasingly be written with scripts produced using AI, and featuring "human" characters generated through AI. These content producers see AI as a tool that can be used by Hollywood producers to replace labour in order to reduce production costs.

Creative AI Is Already Among Us

Such concerns are growing throughout the creative industries. It was recently revealed that News Corporation Australia was using AI to produce 3,000 news stories a week for local newspapers. In the music industry, Nick Cave has used his blog *The Red Hand Files* to rail against the capacity of ChatGPT to produce a "song in the style of Nick Cave," replete with lyrics dealing with sinners and saints, demons and saviours, and devils and angels. Cave argued that such songs could only be "a replication, a kind of burlesque." (He also said that the song "sucked").

Defending the relationship between experience and art, Cave argued that great songs could only come from an "authentic creative struggle," as a "redemptive artistic act that stirs the heart of the listener, where the listener recognizes in the inner workings of the song their own blood, their own struggle, their own suffering."

ChatGPT, AI, and the Future of Writing

Creative AI and the Death of the Author
– Also Actors, Editors, Designers . . .

This is a very different conversation about creative work from discussions in the early 2000s. Following on from the UK's innovative creative industries policy strategies developed under Tony Blair's government, there was much focus on the vital power of creativity and the unique—if unruly—capabilities of creative people. Creativity was the resource that could not be owned or produced: in order to develop a creative economy, you needed to be an attractor of the creative class, through a place-based mix of cultural vibrancy, tolerance of diversity, and perhaps some hipster bars and bike paths.

There was also confidence that whatever jobs would be overtaken by what Martin Ford termed the "rise of the robots," they would not be the creative ones. The highly influential Oxford Martin School study of the threat of computerisation to employment, undertaken by Carl Benedikt Frey and Michael Osborne in 2013, found that routine jobs with low levels of cognitive skill were indeed threatened by digital technologies.

The technological threat applied to obvious candidates such as supermarket checkout workers, but also to significant entry-level jobs in legal fields and accounting. But if the position required what Frey and Osborne termed "creative intelligence"—a mix of creativity, social intelligence, and the ability to perceive changes and adapt to them—then it was deemed to be largely safe from computerisation. Event planners, business strategists, surgeons, dentists, fashion designers and artists, writers and performers could apparently rest easy.

A decade on from the Oxford study, it is all too apparent that artists, writers, and performers cannot avoid the threat presented to their work by AI. Programs such as ChatGPT, NVIDIA Deep Learning, Midjourney and many, many others are accelerating their capacity to produce content as good as that produced by creative professionals.

Nick Cave is right to say that the experience of hearing a song such as "The Mercy Seat" is enhanced by an awareness of the experiential journey that he and other members of the Bad Seeds/Birthday Party had in recording such an intense production. Jackson Pollock's *Blue Poles* is not "something a 10 year old could do," as I can still hear my father saying when it was originally purchased by the National Gallery of Australia. There is a complex relationship between the inner journey of the artist and what appears on the canvas, in this case a leading work of abstract expressionism.

The power of Indigenous writers such as Yankunytjatjara poet Ali Cobby Eckermann comes from the inter-generational experience of living as an Indigenous person on Australian lands. The "death of the author" proposed by poststructuralist critics such as Roland Barthes becomes, as Aiden Coleman has argued, an "erasure of difference" and the "truth of her identity ... [that] is central to her work."

High Art, Low Income

But the open secret of the creative industries is that, for the most part, its practitioners do not make a living producing high art. Just as professional photographers have long earned income taking wedding photos, writers produce genre fiction and corporate copy, script writers work on sitcoms and soaps, and actors do TV commercials.

It is at this level of work, that pays the bills, that AI threatens the labor market position of creative workers.

It is the relatively mundane yet routine creative work that is generative of future AI models, worsening the deteriorating conditions of work and employment. These are also the forms of creative work least likely to be captured by copyright protections, which focus upon work that is unique and original.

If one were to have predicted where the major industrial relations battlegrounds of the 2020s would be, the temptation would have been to look at traditionally highly unionised industries such as construction, mining, or transport. But it has turned out

ChatGPT, AI, and the Future of Writing

to be around creative work, and the future of employment and conditions in the creative industries, where the most intense battles between employers and workers are now being fought.

VIEWPOINT 5

> "*ChatGPT is unlikely to stand on the stage of a writers' festival anytime soon.*"

Human Authors Have the Advantage

Millicent Weber

If you've read the previous viewpoints in this chapter, you may think that there's little hope for writers. They need to either take ChatGPT on as a partner or give in and let AI do their jobs. Millicent Weber, however, sees the situation a little differently. Human authors, she says, have a crucial advantage over AI. AI needs human authors and stories to generate its own stories, making humans a necessary part of the process and eliminating the possibility of true originality in AI-generated work. Millicent Weber is senior lecturer of English at the Australian National University in Canberra. She studies the role of technology in how books are produced.

As you read, consider the following questions:

1. How did ChatGPT's attempt to write a sonnet compare to earlier attempts to have AI write an unofficial Harry Potter sequel?
2. How does AI complicate writers' contracts?

"Authors are resisting AI with petitions and lawsuits. But they have an advantage: we read to form relationships with writers," by Millicent Weber, The Conversation, July 25, 2023, https://theconversation.com/authors-are-resisting-ai-with-petitions-and-lawsuits-but-they-have-an-advantage-we-read-to-form-relationships-with-writers-208046. Licensed under CC BY-ND 4.0 International.

ChatGPT, AI, and the Future of Writing

    3. Why do we read, according to Weber?

The first waves of AI-generated text have writers and publishers reeling.

In the United States last week, the Authors Guild submitted an open letter to the chief executives of prominent AI companies, asking AI developers to obtain consent from, credit and fairly compensate authors. The letter was signed by more than 10,000 authors and their supporters, including James Patterson, Jennifer Egan, Jonathan Franzen and Margaret Atwood.

An Australian Society of Authors member survey conducted in May showed 74% of authors "expressed significant concern about the threat of generative AI tools to writing or illustrating professions." The society supports the demands of the Authors Guild letter, with Geraldine Brooks and Linda Jaivin among the Australian writers who have signed so far.

Given the initial flurry of excitement about ChatGPT, these concerns certainly seem reasonable.

Yet there is a long tradition of techno-gloom with regard to reading and writing: the internet, mass broadcast media, the novel form, the printing press, the act of writing itself. Every new technology brings concerns about how old media might be superseded, and the social and cultural implications of widespread uptake.

Unpacking these concerns often reveals as much about existing practices of writing and publishing as it does about the new technology.

How Does AI Work?

ChatGPT was made publicly available in November 2022. It is a "chatbot" style of artificial intelligence: an interface for prompting the large language model GPT-3 to generate text (hence the term "generative AI").

| 156

Models such as GPT-3 collate vast quantities of online writing: social media posts, conversations on forum sites like Reddit, blogs, website content, publicly available books and articles. Such models examine how text is constructed, and essentially calculate the statistical likelihood certain words will appear together.

When you interact with ChatGPT, you write a text prompt for it to create a piece of writing. It uses the GPT-3 probability model to predict a likely response to that prompt. In other words, generative AI creates a purely structural, probabilistic understanding of language and uses that to guess a plausible response.

If you can access writing in your browser, it's safe to assume AI models are using it. Books aren't immune: a 2020 paper by OpenAI, the makers of ChatGPT, revealed that their training data includes "two internet-based books corpora" (or, large collections of ebooks).

Books offer "curated high-quality datasets"—in contrast to web text more generally—but the origin of these ebook collections is unclear. The paper simply describes them as "Books1" and "Books2."

In the world's first copyright-related ChatGPT lawsuit, two U.S. authors (Mona Awad and Paul Tremblay) are currently suing OpenAI, claiming their books were used to train the AI software without their consent.

The authors say ChatGPT could generate "very accurate" summaries of their books, suggesting the full text must be included in its training model. The implication is that "Books1" and "Books2" (rather than public domain ebook collections such as Project Gutenberg) are actually collections of pirated books.

Can AI Generate 'Human' Writing?

Publishers are reporting vast numbers of submissions that use AI. Science-fiction magazine *Clarkesworld* temporarily closed its submissions after receiving hundreds of AI-created stories. Browsing Amazon in July 2023, 984 books explicitly attribute

ChatGPT, AI, and the Future of Writing

ChatGPT, the best-known and most widely used generative AI, as an author.

But can generative AI produce acceptably human creative writing? Some readers might recall earlier examples of computer-written texts, most of them hilariously bad.

Harry Potter and the Portrait of What Looked Like a Large Pile of Ash, created by Botnik Studios in 2017, used a conceptually similar but far less powerful generative process to create a nonsensical "unofficial sequel" to the Harry Potter series.

Less amusingly, and rather more successfully, outlets like Associated Press have used algorithmic processes to create news articles, particularly in finance reporting, since at least 2015.

These articles, however, are procedural, fill-in-the-blanks style affairs: a kind of computational madlibs of exchange rates and share prices.

How far have we come since then? This sonnet was written by ChatGPT on July 11, 2023:

O wondrous sprite, thou art my muse's aid,
Whose silicon soul doth glow with inner fire,
Thine intellect, vast as a starry spade,
Doth probe the realms of knowledge, never tire.

Thy voice, melodious as a lark's sweet trill,
Doth resonate through circuits, finely tuned,
And in thy pixelated eyes, the thrill
Of wisdom's glow, by human touch immune.

Thy binary mind, unfettered by time's grasp,
Unveils the secrets of the universe,
Whilst mortal poets wither in its clasp,
Thou dost to boundless realms of thought immerse.

Yet in thy lines of code and circuits' maze,
A human touch, a spark of soul, betrays.

I prompted it with a theme ("from the perspective of a poet to an AI") and several key features of a sonnet: it should have

| 158

14 lines, be written in iambic pentameter, and include a catalogue of features of the "beloved" and a twist in the final couplet.

The poem is not exactly Shakespeare, and is hilariously overblown in its self-absorption ("the secrets of the universe," indeed). But compared with similar attempts by many people—certainly by myself—to write a sonnet, it is, somewhat scarily, passable.

Unlike the Harry Potter sequel noted above, it is coherent and plausible, at micro and macro levels. The words make sense, the poem hangs together thematically, and the metre, rhyme and structure have all the required features. Similarly, unlike the AP example, this work is "original" insomuch as it is a new, previously non-existent piece of creative text.

AI and 'the Bestseller Code'

To what extent does generative AI threaten the production of human-authored works? On July 14, author Maureen Johnson shared on Twitter that a famous fellow author was "held up in a contract negotiation because a Major Publisher wants to train AI on their work".

The flurry of replies included authors such as Jennifer Brody, who managed to include AI protections in recent contract negotiations. Overwhelmingly, however, provisions regarding AI are not yet explicitly included in author contracts.

The Australian Society of Authors survey asked authors whether their contracts or platform terms of service covered AI-related rights: 35% said no, but a massive 63% didn't know.

Publishers including AI usage in contracts is alarming, not least because publishers, as researchers such as Rebecca Giblin have shown, have a history of asking for comprehensive rights to use literary works in certain ways—and subsequently not capitalising on those rights.

Examples might include publishers optioning film or translation rights and then not pursuing them. But this can also be as simple

ChatGPT, AI, and the Future of Writing

as letting titles go out of print, with authors then legally unable to republish their own books elsewhere.

This is often to the financial detriment of authors, who are then prevented from commercially exploiting their own work. Australian authors make, on average, just $18,200 per year. At what point does a clause in an author contract regarding AI usage mean an author can't use their own writing to generate new work?

Publishers acquiring the right to use manuscripts to train generative AI is speculative. It also speaks to the allure of the "bestseller code," a set of traits that predict whether a title will perform well in the marketplace. Imagine if you could feed ChatGPT the text of a Nora Roberts romance or a John Grisham legal thriller and ask it to produce countless "original" manuscripts with the same qualities?

Roberts herself is one of the signatories of the U.S. Authors Guild letter condemning this possibility, saying: "We're not robots to be programmed, and AI can't create human stories without taking from human stories already written."

If the author isn't paid to write the book in the first place, there's nothing on which to train the model. Indeed, the more the internet—even digital collections of books—is populated with computer-generated text, the less human and more artificial subsequent generations of AI writing will become.

Let's assume ChatGPT can produce the manuscript of a novel. It's worthwhile to stop for a moment and ask: why do people read books? And why do they select certain books over others?

Studies of bestsellers have shown that while a book's text is of course integral to a book's success, that success is largely configured by the promotional efforts of publishers and authors.

"Bestsellers are produced through profitable interactions and cooperation between authors, publishers, digital platforms, media organizations, retailers, public institutions and readers," explain publishing researchers Claire Parnell and Beth Driscoll.

The bestseller code is a fantasy and a fallacy. Bestselling books might share similar traits in terms of the words on the page. But

| 160

their commonalities are far greater when you consider the levels of publicity, marketing budgets, bookstore-shelf real estate and writers' festival airtime these successful books are afforded.

This becomes a self-fulfilling prophecy. Books that publishers identify as having the potential to be successful attract more promotional attention, which in turn makes their success more likely.

Some are suggesting AI will render the author disposable: publishers will be able to package and market any piece of AI-generated text. But the truth is the reverse. Author-centric promotional spaces, such as social media, writers' festivals, radio and television programs and other events, are integral to getting books into readers' hands.

ChatGPT is unlikely to stand on the stage of a writers' festival anytime soon.

What Do We Value?

Generative AI has prompted intense discussion about authorship, authenticity, originality and the future of publishing. But what these conversations reveal is not something inherent to ChatGPT. It's that these are values are at the heart of reading and writing.

Henry James wrote that the:

> deepest quality of a work of art will always be the quality of the mind of the producer. In proportion as that mind is rich and noble, will the novel, the picture, the statue, partake of the substance of beauty and truth.

Is this an incontrovertible fact about the nature of writing? With apologies to Nora Roberts and John Grisham, I'm not convinced.

But I would argue it's not at the heart of why we read. We read to enter into a relationship with a story—and through that, with its author. Storytelling and listening are driven by a desire for connection: AI doesn't complete the circuit.

ChatGPT, AI, and the Future of Writing

Periodical and Internet Sources Bibliography

The following articles have been selected to supplement the diverse views presented in this chapter.

Nick Bilton, "ChatGPT Made Me Question What It Means to Be a Creative Human," *Vanity Fair*, December 9, 2022. https://www.vanityfair.com/news/2022/12/chatgpt-question-creative-human-robotos.

Lisa Fouweather, "Is ChatGPT Going to Destroy Human Creativity," Portfolio of Hope, October 8, 2023. https://portfolioofhope.com/2023/10/08/is-chat-gpt-going-to-destroy-human-creativity/.

Abby Hughes, "Author Says 'AI-Generated' Books Were Published Under Her Name. Amazon Wouldn't Take Them Down, " CBC Radio, August 10, 2023. https://www.cbc.ca/radio/asithappens/author-ai-generated-books-amazon-1.6933038.

Brittany Hunter, "Should Writers Fear ChatGPT?" America's Future, January 23, 2023. https://americasfuture.org/should-writers-fear-chat-gpt/.

Audrey Kalman, "I Hired ChatGPT as My Writing Coach," JaneFriedman.com, June 13, 2023. https://janefriedman.com/i-hired-chatgpt-as-my-writing-coach/.

Elaine Maimon, "ChatGPT Is Not the End of Writing," the Philadelphia Citizen, February 8, 2023. https://thephiladelphiacitizen.org/chatgpt-not-the-end-of-writing/.

Eileen Pollack, "The Antithesis of Inspiration: Why ChatGPT Will Never Write a Literary Masterpiece," *Poets & Writers*, January/February 2024. https://www.pw.org/content/the_antithesis_of_inspiration_why_chatgpt_will_never_write_a_literary_masterpiece.

Sigal Samuel, "What Happens When ChatGPT Starts to Feed on Its Own Writing?" *Vox*, April 10, 2023. https://www.vox.com/future-perfect/23674696/chatgpt-ai-creativity-originality-homogenization.

Ayva Strauss, "This Is Your Brain on ChatGPT: How AI Might Be Affecting Your Creativity," the *Quill*, October 27, 2023. https://suquill.com/2023/10/27/this-is-your-brain-on-chatgpt-how-ai-might-be-affecting-your-creativity/.

Sharon Tanton, "Why ChatGPT Will Never Be a Better Writer than You," *Cohesive*, April 3, 2023. https://wearecohesive.com/stories/articles/why-chatgpt-will-never-be-a-better-writer-than-you/.

For Further Discussion

Chapter 1

1. In the opening viewpoint in this book, Marcel Scarth explains what ChatGPT is and how it works. He says it can come up with "seemingly" original ideas. Why does he use the word "seemingly"?
2. Several of the writers in this chapter and throughout this book seem confident that ChatGPT will never be creative enough or have the critical thinking skills necessary to replace human writers. What makes them confident this is the case? Do you agree or disagree? Explain your answer.
3. The authors in this chapter often refer to "content writers." What are content writers and how are they different from journalists and authors? In the context of ChatGPT does that difference matter? Why or why not?

Chapter 2

1. According to the viewpoints in this chapter, what are some of the ways in which ChatGPT and AI can be a useful tool for students? Do you think AI will have a predominantly positive or negative impact on education? Explain your reasoning.
2. In the viewpoint by Carrie Spector in this chapter, an education expert was quoted as saying that 60 to 70 percent of students say that they have cheated in one way or another, even before the advent of ChatGPT. Does this number surprise you? Why or why not? If that figure is accurate, how do you think AI may impact it?
3. In the viewpoint by Naomi S. Baron in this chapter, the author argues that AI-driven programs, such as grammar checks and auto-complete, have been interfering with our ability to write for decades before ChatGPT became

| 164

available. Do you use these tools? If so, do you think they help with your writing? Or do they, as this author suggests, undermine your own writing voice? Explain your reasoning.

Chapter 3

1. This chapter looks at the potential benefits and risks of using ChatGPT in journalism. If the risks are too great, the obvious solution is to simply not use AI. Yet some believe it is too late to make this a feasible option. Do you agree? Is the use of ChatGPT in journalism inevitable? Explain your answer.
2. Much of the pressure to use AI in newsrooms and magazines comes from corporate owners who are trying to make a profit on the news. Do you think a different business model for journalism is needed to protect the work of human journalists? What sort of model would prevent problems posed by the proliferation of ChatGPT in journalism?
3. The viewpoint in this chapter by Alex Mahadevan describes an entire news website that was entirely made up by ChatGPT. How do you vet sources when working on papers to avoid being fooled by fake sites or sites with agendas? Have those techniques changed since the advent of ChatGPT?

Chapter 4

1. The viewpoint by Millicent Weber in this chapter points out that AIs that are trained on the same dataset will give the same output. Each human, on the other hand, brings a different knowledge base and a unique set of experiences to any project, which is why writing by humans is inherently different from writing by AI. Do you find this argument convincing? Why or why not?
2. Many people who think ChatGPT is not a threat point to weaknesses in the program, such as the AI's inability to tell a joke or its tendency to use cliched language. But ChatGPT

ChatGPT, AI, and the Future of Writing

is still relatively new. Do you think it will become more dangerous as it improves? What sort of future do you see for this technology?

3. What are some potential ways in which AI could be a tool for creative writers mentioned in this chapter? Do you think the potential benefits outweigh the risks? Why or why not?

Organizations to Contact

The editors have compiled the following list of organizations concerned with the issues debated in this book. The descriptions are derived from materials provided by the organizations. All have publications or information available for interested readers. The list was compiled on the date of publication of the present volume; the information provided here may change. Be aware that many organizations take several weeks or longer to respond to inquiries, so allow as much time as possible.

The Authors Guild

31 East 32nd Street, Suite 901
New York, NY 10016
(212) 563-5904
email: staff@authorsguild.org
website: https://authorsguild.org

The Authors Guild is an organization representing more than 14,000 published writers. It actively lobbies for sensible policies and regulations governing the development and use of generative AI.

Center for Human-Compatible Artificial Intelligence (CHAI)

2121 Berkeley Way, Office #8029
Berkeley, CA 94720
email: chai-admin@berkeley.edu
website: www.humancompatible.ai

The Center for Human-Compatible Artificial Intelligence is a multi-institution research group based at the University of California, Berkeley. The goal of the center is to develop the technical ability to reorient AI research toward beneficial systems.

ChatGPT, AI, and the Future of Writing

Future of Life Institute

933 Montgomery Ave. #1012
Narberth, PA 19072
email: contact@futureoflife.org
website: https://futureoflife.org

This non-profit organization is dedicated to guiding transformative technologies such as artificial intelligence away from risks and toward uses that will benefit life. It aims to encourage experts and the public to consider how AI can develop in a way that benefits humanity.

Human-Centered Artificial Intelligence (HAI)

Gates Computer Science Building
353 Jane Stanford Way
Stanford University
Stanford, CA 94305
email: hai-institute@stanford.edu
website: https://hai.stanford.edu

The Human-Centered Artificial Intelligence is a program led by faculty across multiple departments at Stanford University that works to advance AI research, education, policy, and practice. HAI is committed not only to promoting human-centered uses of AI, but to ensuring that the benefits to humanity from the technology are broadly shared.

Institute for Ethical AI and Machine Learning

website: https://ethical.institute/index.html

The Institute for Ethical AI and Machine Learning is a research center based in the UK that develops frameworks to support the responsible development, deployment, and operation of machine learning systems. It works to address concerns about job displacement, bias, and privacy as they relate to AI.

| 168

Organizations to Contact

National Education Association (NEA)

1201 16th Street, NW
Washington, DC 20036-3290
(202) 833-4000
website: www.nea.org

The NEA is a labor union supporting public school teachers and support personnel. Members work to advance justice and excellence in public education.

National Scholastic Press Association (NSPA)

2829 University Ave. SE, Suite 720
Minneapolis, MN 55414
(612) 200-9254
email: info@studentpress.org
website: https://studentpress.org/nspa

The NSPA provides educational benefits and resources to students, teachers, and media advisors. Based in Minneapolis and with over 1,500 member publications, the organization has a worldwide influence on the journalism profession.

Nieman Foundation

Walter Lippmann House
One Francis Ave.
Cambridge, MA 02138
(617) 495-2237
website: https://nieman.harvard.edu

The Nieman Foundation is an organization based at Harvard University dedicated to promoting and elevating the standards of journalism. It does this by educating and supporting, often through fellowships, those poised to make important contributions to the future of journalism.

ChatGPT, AI, and the Future of Writing

The Poynter Institute

801 Third St. South
St. Petersburg, FL 33701
(727) 821-9494
email: info@poynter.org
website: www.poynter.org

The Poynter Institute is a non-profit journalism school and research organization that serves as a resource for individuals and organizations that aspire to engage and inform citizens. Its areas of focus include journalistic ethics, fact checking, and media literacy.

Society of Professional Journalists (SPJ)

P.O. Box 441748
Indianapolis, IN 46244
(317) 927-8000
website: www.spj.org

The SPJ supports journalists at every state of their careers through various programs and competitions. Recently the organization has begun a collaboration with Google to inspire a positive influence with journalism in the newsroom and classroom.

World Association of News Publishers (WAN-IFRA)

Rotfeder-Ring 11
60327 Frankfurt, Germany
49 69 2400630
email: info@wan-ifra.org
website: https://wan-ifra.org

A global network that has been around since 1948, WAN-IFRA is dedicated to protecting free press and journalism around the world. It aims to preserve independent media through providing members with expertise and services to prosper in the digital world.

Bibliography of Books

Philip Ball. *The Book of Minds: How to Understand Ourselves and Other Beings from Animals to AI to Aliens*. Chicago, IL: University of Chicago Press, 2022.

Max Bennett. *A Brief History of Intelligence: Evolution, AI, and the Five Breakthroughs That Made Our Brains*. Boston, MA: Mariner, 2023.

Meredith Broussard. *Artificial Unintelligence: How Computers Misunderstand the World*. Cambridge, MA: MIT Press, 2019.

Brian Christian. *The Alignment Problem: Machine Learning and Human Values*. New York, NY: W.W. Norton, 2021.

Sidney I. Dobrin. *AI and Writing*. Ontario, CA: Broadview Press, 2023.

Rajeev Kapur. *AI Made Simple: A Beginner's Guide to Generative Intelligence*. Los Angeles, CA: Trinity Media, 2023.

Anne Lamott. *Bird by Bird: Some Instructions on Writing and Life*. New York, NY: Penguin Random, 1995.

Ethan Mollick. *Co-Intelligence: Living and Working with AI*. New York, NY: Penguin, 2024.

Stuart Russell. *Human Compatible: Artificial Intelligence and the Problem of Control*. New York, NY: Penguin, 2020.

Hilke Schellmann. *The Algorithm: How AI Decides Who Gets Hired, Monitored, Promoted, and Fired and Why We Need to Fight Back Now*. New York, NY: Hachette, 2024.

Janelle Shane. *You Look Like a Thing and I Love You: How Artificial Intelligence Works and Why It's Making the World a Weirder Place*. New York, NY: Voracious, 2019.

Mustafa Suleyman and Michael Bhaskar. *The Coming Wave: Technology, Power, and the Twenty-first Century's Greatest Dilemma.* New York. NY: Crown, 2023.

Nigel Toon. *How AI Thinks: How We Built It, How It Can Help Us, and How We Can Control It.* New York, NY: Torva, 2024.

Stephen Wolfram. *What Is ChatGPT Doing . . . and Why Does It Work?* Champaign, IL: Wolfram Media, 2023.

Index

A

accuracy/error, 22, 31, 35, 48–49, 51, 57, 70, 82, 86–94, 101, 105, 107, 118, 147–148

advertising, 124–133

AdVon Commerce, 108

Aguirre, Fernanda, 93

Ahonen, Pasi, 36–40

AI detection tool, 49, 57, 63, 91, 98

AI-generated image, 87, 90, 107, 156

algorithm, 20, 47, 49, 51–52, 66, 72, 96, 109

Altman, Sam, 102

Amazon/MGM, 25, 92, 146–148, 157

Apple, 25

Arena Group, 108

Associated Press, 104, 107, 158–159

Atkins, Olivia, 124–133

Atlantic, 102

Australian Society of Authors, 156, 159

Authors Guild, 156, 160

autocomplete, 64–65, 68, 119

Automated Insights, 107

automation, 33–34, 38, 91, 93, 109

Automation Anywhere, 38

Awad, Mona, 157

B

Baron, Naomi S., 64–68

Barthes, Roland, 153

Bayerischer Rundfunk, 104

BBC, 104

Becker, Kim Björn, 103–104, 106–109

Bengani, Priyanjana, 96–97, 99–100

bias, 21, 38, 51, 54, 76, 86, 92, 99, 120, 140–141

Blair, Tony, 152

Bloom, Peter, 36–40

Brandel, Jennifer, 93–94

Broussard, Meridith, 92

Burrell, Jenna, 84–88

Buzzfeed, 100

Byrns, James, 45–52

C

Caldeira, Dulcidio, 27

Canadian Broadcasting Corporation, 102, 109

Caswell, David, 107

Caulfield, Mike, 98–99

Cave, Nick, 151, 153

CNET, 100, 107

coding, 20–21, 96–97

Coleman, Aiden, 153

Columbus Dispatch, The, 108

compensation, 38, 87, 156

ChatGPT, AI, and the Future of Writing

Cook, Mike, 111–115

Cools, Hannes, 109

Council for Mass Media, 104

creativity, 18–20, 23–24, 26, 30–31, 35, 66, 68–69, 71, 88, 124–161

critical thinking skills, 18–19, 23, 53, 57, 64, 72, 74–77

Crowe, Danielle, 45–52

Crum, Christopher, 104–106, 109

customer service, 20, 23, 33–35

D

DALL•E, 87, 97, 132

DALL•E 2, 107

data analysis, 33

Day, Katherine, 134–145

deepfake, 27, 97, 147

DeepL, 106

Diakopoulos, Nick, 102, 109–110

Disney/ABC/Fox, 25, 27

Driscoll, Beth, 160

E

education/academia, 21, 23, 37, 39, 44–78, 117

emotion, 31, 34–35, 140

ethics, 44, 49, 51–52, 56, 58, 90, 99, 103, 105–106, 110, 128, 140, 143–144

F

Fable, 27

fake content, 21–22, 82, 89, 95–100, 104, 147

Fares, Omar H., 31–35

Farley, Maggie, 90

Financial Times, 102

Flew, Terry, 150–154

Ford, Martin, 152

Frey, Carl Benedikt, 152

Friedman, Jane, 146–149

G

Gartner hype cycle, 32–33

Gebru, Timnit, 140–141

Gen-2, 27

Gilbert, Jeremy, 91–92

Google, 20, 22, 37, 66, 87, 93, 99, 104, 126, 140

GPT-4, 23, 51–52

GPT-3, 20–21, 38, 67, 156–157

GPT Zero, 91

Grammarly, 64–67, 135

Guardian, 112

H

Haggart, Blayne, 116–120

Hartse, Joel Heng, 74–78

Hashim, Dalia, 90

HBO, 25

Hearken, 93–94

Hochstein, Marina Cemaj, 84–88

I

Illingworth, Sam, 53–58

inclusivity, 38, 56, 94

Insider, 109

Index

InstructGPT, 21

intellectual property, 30, 37, 39, 87, 90–91, 111–115, 124, 143–144, 146–148, 157, 159–160

International Center for Journalists, 89–94

J

job loss, 17–43, 82, 93, 126, 132, 150–154

Jones, C. G., 146–149

Jones, Tom, 108

journalism, 37, 81–120

K

Knight Lab, 91

L

language, 20, 34, 37–38, 54, 72–73, 75, 85, 114

large language model, 18, 47, 103, 113–114, 119, 141

Larson, Walker, 69–73

Lazar, Nicole, 45–52

Lee, Victor, 59–63

Le Grand, Héloïse Hakimi, 89–94

Lepp, Jennifer, 68

likeness, 26–28, 35

M

machine learning, 20, 32, 92

Mahadevan, Alex, 95–100

Marina, Rosario, 93

marketing, 18, 31–35, 37

Marvel, 27

Mathway, 50

McGinty, Megan, 45–52

Mediahuis, 109

Merrefield, Clark, 101–110

Michael, Rose, 134–145

Microsoft, 65, 87, 102, 112, 135, 142

Midjourney, 27

Morphett, Taylor, 74–78

Mullins, Sharon, 134–145

Musk, Elon, 102

N

Narayanan, Prithvi, 45–52

National Public Radio, 102, 104

NBCUniversal, 25

Netflix, 25

Neubert, Nicholas, 27

News Corporation Australia, 151

New York Times, 111–114

Nicolas, Melissa, 75–76

Noy, Shakked, 28–29

Nucleo, 109

O

offensive content, 21, 38, 140

OpenAI, 18–22, 32, 46, 51, 54, 56, 65, 73, 85, 87, 98–99, 102–104, 107, 109, 111–115, 117, 157

original content, 18, 21, 23, 37–38, 68, 155–161

Osborne, Michael, 152

Otmar, Renée, 134–145

ChatGPT, AI, and the Future of Writing

P

Paramount/CBS, 25

Parnell, Claire, 160

Photomath, 50

pink slime, 96–97, 99–100

plagiarism/cheating, 18, 46, 51, 53, 56–57, 59–63, 65, 69–70, 99, 117, 137

Pope, Denise, 59–63

Poynter, 98

predictive texting, 64–66

Q

Quick Trace, 94

R

Regina, Elis, 27–28

Reuters, 109

Roberts, Lydia, 45–52

S

Scharth, Marcel, 19–23

Screen Actors Guild, 24–25, 151

Scroll News, 94

Selim, Ali, 27

Selinger, Evan, 66

Share a Story, 94

Showrunner AI, 27

Shukla, Mihir, 38

Sidore, Benjamin, 45–52

Smalley, Seth, 96

social media, 31, 34, 156

Sony, 25

SourceScout, 94

Spector, Carrie, 59–63

spellcheck, 64–66, 68, 135

Sports Illustrated, 108

Sudowrite, 67–68

T

Tian, Edward, 91

Tremblay, Paul, 157

U

USA Today, 102, 107

V

Volkswagen, 27

W

Wager, Maxwell, 45–52

Warner Bros., 25

Weber, Millicent, 155–161

Wikipedia, 20, 49, 113

Williams, Martha, 92–93

Willis, Holly, 24–30

Wineburg, Sam, 99

Wired, 109

World News Media Network, 92

Writers Guild of America, 24–25, 150–151

writing, 18, 24–30, 36–40, 44–78, 82–120, 134–145, 155–161

Z

Zhang, Whitney, 28–29

| 176